A DAUGHTER OF THE MEDICI
And Other Stories

A DAUGHTER OF THE MEDICI
AND OTHER STORIES

BY
DONN BYRNE (1889-1928)

Short Story Index Reprint Series

 BOOKS FOR LIBRARIES PRESS
FREEPORT, NEW YORK

First Published 1935
Reprinted 1970

STANDARD BOOK NUMBER:
8369-3574-8

LIBRARY OF CONGRESS CATALOG CARD NUMBER:
73-125207

PRINTED IN THE UNITED STATES OF AMERICA

CONTENTS

		PAGE
I.	A Daughter of The Medici	1
II.	Champions	26
III.	A Happy Ending	56
IV.	A Certain Regrettable Occasion	79
V.	Anti-Climax	100
VI.	The Cock and Bull Story of Captain Patrick Burgoyne	126
VII.	The Evil Men Do	147
VIII.	As to Impediments	193
IX.	Harley Johnston, Gentleman	213

I

A DAUGHTER OF THE MEDICI

She sat in the office of the big bank's president, tall, stately as a queen, with her face that was more noble than beautiful, like that of the wife of some doge of Venice; and her beautiful slim hands were before her, like resting butterflies.

Brainerd, the bulky bank president, deferred to her as to royalty.

"Signorina Coselschi," he said, "you haven't told me yet why you are in America. We had heard you were married, and were directing the bank with your husband's aid. We shouldn't call you Coselschi at all, but your father's name is so well known."

"Yes, I am married," she smiled, but she gave no information as to her husband's name. Her voice was very musical—very cultured, as the adjective goes—and her marked foreign accent was like a Neapolitan song. "Tell me," she asked. "You know of everyone in the banking business in New York. Do you know of an Italian who came here within a year or so, named Aldo Cesi—a Genoese?"

A DAUGHTER OF THE MEDICI

"Can't place the name."

"A short, compact man; speaks English not at all; very olive complexion, and dark eyes, and beautiful teeth; wears a moustache turned upward at the corners—a very good-looking man, dresses extremely well?"

"The only one I can think of is Giulio Caracci, with the Keene National Bank—rather a bounder, I think, and something of a cheap dandy."

He did not notice that she lowered her magnificent head at his words, hiding a sudden hard resentment.

"You don't know, of course, if he has a birthmark, a red spot about the size of a soldo, on his left cheek?"

"He has," Brainerd nodded emphatically.

She made no sign of relief or displeasure but changed the conversation back to banking matters, and as she talked business the bluff American marvelled. He had always heard of the Coselschi, the great Lombard bankers, and indeed once he had met old Giovanni, Donna Gilda's father, in London—of course, that was when Brainerd was a very young man, and Coselschi ranked with Rothschild and Morgan.

Brainerd had known that she was head of the business, and he had always thought it was merely

A DAUGHTER OF THE MEDICI

a nominal control—that wiser heads, indeed the staff itself, managed the Coselschi affairs; but now he knew that was wrong. The magnificent woman before him knew banking better than he—had a finer, bigger grasp of the essentials and ideals and possibilities of it, though he knew its detail.

"Your father, Miss Coselschi, had a great grip on Abyssinia——"

She smiled. She looked at her slim, beautiful hands before her, like resting butterflies, and looked back at him again. And suddenly, Brainerd understood Catherine de' Medici, and Catherine of Russia, and the Chinese slave girl who became titular and actual ruler of the Yellow Empire, and he felt very abashed.

She went ahead in her musical, foreign voice that seemed fitted for a Roman drawing-room, and yet strangely fitting here in the atmosphere of finance, asking questions of him, all but cross-examining him on the functions of small country banks; and he regarded her with an admiration into which awe entered.

Her face—her face intrigued him, as the word is. It was so intensely Italian, so racial, and yet so individual. The black hair, the black eyes, the high cheekbones, Amelita Galli-Curci had those; but the singer's face was modern, he felt; that picture of Mona Lisa had the type of face, but she was a wanton woman.

And Gilda Coselschi, he felt, for all her beauty and her foreignness and the passion in her eyes, was a virtuous matron. There was something eternal about her, as about Rome itself. She might have been wife to a Cæsar, with those features, or a splendid Borgia, or a lady at the Court of the Magnificent. "An epic woman," he said to himself.

There ran into his mind a fragment of Botticelli's "Spring," a woman with Gilda Coselschi's face and Gilda Coselschi's figure, small ripe bosom, and great shapely knees. And as he studied, apart, her proud, steadfast eyes and noble mouth, he wondered to himself what manner of woman she would be to love.

A man would be swept out of the annoying detail of life with her; he would have eyes only for the stars and the sea then, and hear in his ears the thunder of the planets. From the looks of her he understood what a man must be to be great.

Well, thank God, he was satisfied, a plain tweed-clad man with a home in Quaker Ridge, and a plump laughing wife with hair the colour of corn and eyes

A DAUGHTER OF THE MEDICI

the blue of cornflowers. He chuckled to himself. He hadn't felt so inconsequential for years.

And, as she rose to go, the thought came into his mind: Who the blazes was Aldo Cesi, or Giulio Caracci, as he called himself now? A cheap guinea, went Brainerd's honest phrase! Why should this daughter of Lombard greatness waste even a thought on him? Hey, why? Ah, yes, that was it! Some absconding bank-clerk she had remembered on her trip to America? Nothing escaped that girl. . . .

She knew enough of New York to understand that she was not going to the best locality when she was riding towards Riverside Drive from her rooms at the Ritz. Were she to live in Manhattan she would have chosen the sedatenesss of Park or Madison Avenue. Riverside Drive, she felt, would be somehow florid, a trifle vulgar—pleasantly so, of course, but—— The car she had taken stopped before a florid apartment house.

"Caracci?" The coloured hall-boy leaned back from the telephone. "Who'll I say?"

She hesitated. Then she gave the name by which all Italy knew her. "Gilda Coselschi."

"Eighth floor." He led her to the elevator.

A small dark woman—a girl, rather—opened the door for her, and Gilda looked at her askance. She was

A DAUGHTER OF THE MEDICI

accustomed to well-trained, silent servants and this one had too confident a manner, too impudent a dress.

"I wanted to see Signor Caracci." About the Italian woman's features there shone a soft, happy light of anticipation.

"Come right in," the girl at the door proffered, "and sit down. I'll tell him. I'm Mrs. Caracci."

Gilda was puzzled.

"I beg your pardon."

"I'm Mrs. Caracci."

She was a dazzling hybrid type, something of the New World, made up like a minor actress. She wore a dress of white satin, and satin shoes, and about her was much jewellery.

"Oh, honey!" she called loudly.

Gilda had become strangely pale. "You said you were Mrs. Caracci?"

"Yeh, I'm Mrs. . . . Caracci."

"But that's impossible," the Lombard lady faltered. "You can't be Mrs. Caracci——"

Caracci came into the ornate sitting-room swaggeringly. Gilda took a step forward.

"Aldo!"

He looked up at her. His face grew blank. Then a sort of silly, uncomprehending smile broke on it. Then it went white.

A DAUGHTER OF THE MEDICI

"Jesus!" he said suddenly, and the perspiration sprang out on his forehead.

"Aldo!" There was shock and horror in Gilda's voice.

The little woman looked at them in amazement.

"What's the idea?" she broke in angrily. "Jule, who is this woman?" She turned to Gilda. "What do you want of him? Who are you, anyway?"

"My poor girl"—Gilda Coselschi had tears of sympathy in her eyes as she looked at her—"I am this man's wife."

"So!" The New York girl looked her up and down. "So!" Her arms went akimbo on her hips and a sort of savage light of battle came into her eyes. "Well, poor nothin'! Le' me tell you somethin'. I'm married to this man good, y'understand, good an' fi'm. An' you can quit buttin' in right here an' now—you get me."

She went over to the shivering Genoese and put her arms about him. "Poor honey! Well, I like her cheek, comin' in like this! If you was married to him, why didn't you come over here with him? I'll bet he couldn't live with you." Evidently not; Gilda's heart contracted. "You didn't understand him," the girl drooled over the man, who stood wretched there like a bedraggled peacock. "You had no right to him if you couldn't keep him."

Each word she said dripped acid on the Italian woman's heart. "You can't say he left you without anythin'." She ranged over the subtly simple line of Gilda's frock and her Tappé hat, observed the neatly shod slim and shapely Lombard foot. "He did well by you, but you didn't give him loving enough. Honey boy, I'll stick."

"What are you going to do, Gilda?" Her husband was piteously afraid. "What are you going to do?"

"Yeh, what are you go'n 'o do about it?" rasped the woman.

"You were always good, Gilda," he reminded her. "You were always kind."

"I don't see that there's anything for me to do," Gilda managed to say.

"You go back t' Italy," the woman called Caracci advised. "You see he doesn't want you. What's the use?"

"You wouldn't tell the police, Gilda." He shivered in an ague of cowardice. "You were always so good!"

"You be sensible and go back t' Italy," the girl advised again. "See the way I'm taking it. I didn't know he left a wife behind, but I ain't kicking, am

A DAUGHTER OF THE MEDICI

I? You ain't one of those hatin' Italian women, I can see that; you go back and get married again. You can say he's dead."

"You wouldn't tell the police," Cesi pleaded again.

"It will not be I who will inform the police; I promise you that," said Gilda Coselschi, and she left the room and the house, slowly, dignifiedly, very like a queen.

Of course, she had only herself to blame. People used to warn her against him.

"This Aldo Cesi whom you have taken up so much, Gilda," her friends used to say to her, "you know—well, he's rather impossible——"

"I am going to marry Signor Cesi," Gilda had answered haughtily.

"Oh, I beg your pardon." And there it had ended.

She remembered him when he had become associated with her father's business in Florence, dapper, rather ill-bred, pretentious, very eager to please, occasionally dropping into a horrifying vulgarity.

But Cesi was a financial genius—one of those comets that arise in finance out of the gutter, flaming past the embarrassed stars. He was so great that, in recognition of his ability, he was admitted as guest to the Coselschi household, so important was he in the Coselschi bank.

A DAUGHTER OF THE MEDICI

In commerce in Italy there is no greater name than Coselschi. Coselschi—that is all! They might have been dukes, had they wished, but they were greater than dukes. They might have been princes, but they needed no label to proclaim an evident nobility. Their name extends back to the Crusaders, and was notable before then. When Christendom rose to rescue the Tomb, many an Italian nobleman's equipment came from the Coselschi strongbox. Urbino and Lorenzo had been helped by them, and many a Pope. Knights went to them, not as to a tradesman, with a condescending hostility, but as equals giving only their unbreakable word of honour.

In this atmosphere Gilda Coselschi had been reared, accustomed to a code of nobility as high as a medieval knight's: to trust and be trusted, to love Italy, never to break her word, to be gentle towards the poor.

She had a great home and to her came great people, to the palace where a doge of old-time Venice might have lived, a decorous, ascetically luxurious house. Robert Browning had loved that place under the reign of a former Coselschi, and D'Annunzio was happy visiting her father Amadeo—a house of noble shadows and broad spaces where dignified ghosts

A DAUGHTER OF THE MEDICI

might walk by night, past a little known Simonetta of Sandro Botticelli's, past a face by Ghirlandajo, past a statue by John of Athens, and cups that Cellini had hammered. . . . But with none of them had she ever become intimate, as she had suddenly with Aldo Cesi.

There was strange blood in her—blood of women whom the Coselschi of former days had married either through inclination or policy—Hebrew blood, which makes for shrewdness, and Norse blood, which is reckless; Venetian blood, which makes for pride, and Greek blood, which is the ichor of passion; yes, and Turkish blood, too, which is too mysterious to explain.

A tall woman—you can see her in your mind's eye—with a face dark and proud as a Borgia's, though not cruel; with a figure of noble amplitude such as Sandro Botticelli painted in "Spring," and with very tender eyes. Behind those features and form there was a soul of queer, noble elements—a wealth of passion, and notable dreams, ideals high as an Alp.

There were many who loved her for her money when Amadeo, her father, died, and there were a hundred dazzled by her name. And the number who loved her for herself can never be reckoned.

A DAUGHTER OF THE MEDICI

They courted her in plain terms, by rule and convention, nobles, bankers and young poets. For most of them she had admiration and for some affection. But for none of them did she feel the least bit of what she might call love, until she met, and married eventually, Aldo Cesi, who was a gutter-snipe, a bounder, and a fatuous fool.

People were, as a rule, impatient of his manner, his dress, his silly upturned moustache. And they showed it. He was a man who did not belong. His financial genius meant nothing to the sons of Cæsars. To them he was merely a manner of pawnbroker to whom Gilda Coselschi had to be somehow decent.

For her sake they tolerated him. His easy advance was met with polite frigidity. Splendid of heart as she was of presence, Gilda turned to him, was doubly kind and pleasant to him for the affronts he had to suffer. When his presence became intolerable to others, she would draw him aside, into the garden, to some place to show him a picture or a vase, or explain a frieze to him. And she would feel sorry because of his hurt eyes.

"He can't help it, poor little devil," she would protest to her friends. "And he is at bottom the kindest-hearted soul in the world."

A DAUGHTER OF THE MEDICI

"He may be very good to his mother and all that——"

"I think you're all horrible," she would say, and resolve to be kinder than ever to him.

He was always about with her, that small, dapper man, and day by day he grew to mean more to her. She told him about pictures and about life and about manners and she experienced the joy of the priest who instructs a neophyte. And little by little she came to enjoy the eager light in his eyes as he watched her.

He wanted her, and there was no convention of courtship about him. A great lord would waste no time in wooing a girl of the people. Nor would a man of the people wooing a great lady. And when he wanted it, she gave him her heart and body in holy matrimony. Six months later he was gone from her.

"I am not worthy of you, so I am going away," he wrote. "I am not of your world. Good-bye. Aldo." That was all. . . .

To-night in her rooms at the Ritz, giving way to the grief and passion and shame she had felt at the unutterable scene uptown, she saw clearly for the first time since she had known him what manner of man he really was. His vulgarities, his fatuousness, she had ascribed to his lowly origin. "He never had a chance, poor Aldo!" she had always said. She saw now they were natural in him.

He had expected to be put in charge of the Coselschi moneys, to become rich overnight when he married Gilda. That was impossible. The Coselschi affairs were affairs of state, of great names, of idealistic interests, not to be given lightly into the hands of a Genoese adventurer, no matter how shrewd. Aldo wanted to give full vent to that flaming genius of his, so like a Brazilian *rastaqueros*, operating on the rate of exchange, on commodities, on the rise and fall of stocks.

"But, Aldo," she explained, "we Coselschi have bigger ends than personal profit, the good of the country, the interest of the people——"

"But I don't see——"

"You do, Aldo, you do. Down in your heart you understand as well as I do. There is a confidence, dear——"

But it only bored him. He had gone to America to give free rein to his ambitions, and now, following his custom, he was being grounded in preliminary detail of American business as a minor officer in a bank. Soon he would soar.

And she had come after him here believing his note

A DAUGHTER OF THE MEDICI

to be the true explanation: that he felt hurt and small in her surroundings. She had come to comfort and succour him as she had so often done before. And the truth was, he had come across here as any common Calabrian peasant might do, to make his fortune. And he had committed the low peasant's most popular of crimes, which is bigamy.

A great rush of shame consumed her at the memory of the intimacy of her marriage to him. The things she had murmured, abandoning herself to this husband of hers, who was now a strange, vile man! And the thoughts she had dreamed of love and death and eternity, silent and sentient as a tree, while he was there, believing him attuned to her, and he only an obscene outlander in a most sacred fane!

It was as if, liking music, a man had been given a clavichord, with noble line and notes like silver bells, an instrument on which Galuppi might have played his great toccatas, and eventually with shrugging shoulders asked for and got a phonograph with a horn, and a repertoire of tinny records.

O God! . . . And the boast of the family was: they had never been betrayed!

And she, last of the name, a woman of the house, had been fooled and defiled by a fatuous Genoese adventurer. Every thought of him brought a revolting picture into her mind: how he loved luxury, a vulgar luxury, a luxury of hair-oils and no labour; how he would look if he were to get the deserts of his bigamy—the long jail sentence. The oiled head and curled moustache would suffer, the gorgeous haberdashery would be replaced by hideous, coarse grey clothing.

There would be no pleasantries of life in the evening, lights, wine, opera of the more melodious kind, but a damp, odorous, colourless cell, with excessive vermin. And he would labour on stones while guards with rifles watched him. It would kill him, she knew, it would kill him dead. Even were he to emerge, it would be only to crawl back to Genoa, shivering like a rat when the end has come.

But why shouldn't he die, she demanded fiercely, and stood up, eyeing space terribly; why shouldn't he die, not the clean death of a gentleman with steel in his vitals, but a slow, wasting in some fetid hole, for the rat he was? . . . They had never been betrayed! . . . A movement to that telephone, the lifted receiver, a phrase in the mouthpiece. . . . But she had promised she would say nothing to the police of it, and to satisfy him she had given him something greater than the treasures of the Vatican, dearer than life itself to her, the word of a Coselschi!

A DAUGHTER OF THE MEDICI

He would not have gone up to the Plaza to meet Gilda for lunch had he not been afraid to refuse. "I just want to see you, Aldo," she had said on the telephone, and there was neither reproach nor anger in her voice, only a counterpoint of sadness. His hands were wet with perspiration and his heart thumping like a trip-hammer as he followed her and the head waiter to a table.

"I just want to know if you are happy, Aldo." Her deep Lombard eyes questioned him as much as her voice. "Tell me, Aldo, are you happy?"

He could say nothing. This was the last thing he expected.

"Just so that you are happy, that is all I want to know."

And then she turned the conversation, speaking to him of this thing and that, with the old charm, the old habitual grace. She spoke of Italian financial matters, of developments in Somaliland, of new fields in the Argentine. Signor Benelli had written a new play; it was said Gabriele d'Annunzio was at work on a startling novel. The Duke of the Abruzzi was going into the interior of Cambodia.

By a subtle move she lifted him to a station where he had never been before—a social standing where he was the equal of noble Romans. She spoke to

A DAUGHTER OF THE MEDICI

him as though he were an old intimate of her world, now in America. Only occasionally she looked at him out of splendid, tragic eyes, and her mouth quivered as she questioned him.

"Dear Aldo, are you happy?"

With racial histrionic quality he answered neither yes nor no, but something in his dejection was meant to tell her of his misery.

"Poor Aldo! Poor man!"

But for this one reiterated question, she mentioned nothing of their affairs, treating him all the time as an old friend. She electrified him by asking him to show her New York. "I want to see the frivolities," she remarked. And now no longer afraid, but attracted to her strangely, he agreed with eagerness. There was something about the whole thing that intrigued him mightily.

In Italy he had never looked upon her as an especially beautiful woman, somehow, though a thousand other men had. But the night she went with him to the Club de Montmartre she was dazzlingly beautiful and dressed like an empress, and it flattered him tremendously to note the impression she made and the looks cast at him. Unction flowed through his vitals like a warm liquor.

A DAUGHTER OF THE MEDICI

That night going home in a taxi-cab he put his head between his hands and groaned.

"What a fool!" he cried in well-simulated agony. "What a crazy thing to do!"

"Poor Aldo!" Her hand touched his head in benediction. "Poor Aldo! Poor crazy boy!" In the dark he did not notice her contemptuous, sardonic smile.

The situation titillated him. He had often heard of men being good friends with their divorced wives, having lunch with them, accompanying them to the theatre, and that had always struck him as being tremendously of the great world, very high life. And he had introduced a variation of it, very subtle indeed. To be seen with a woman such as she was, beautiful as a star and stately as a queen, about his favourite Broadway resorts—there was ineffable credit and pride to that.

A weekly of a gossipy character, a society sheet in vogue on Broadway, had mentioned her two or three times and had become acquainted with his name and mentioned him, too. It was very flattering. Undoubtedly she was tremendously in love with him, else how, after the affront he had given her, would she have all but wept over him, calling him "Dear Aldo! Poor Aldo!"

A DAUGHTER OF THE MEDICI

Queenie, his new wife, to give her that title, suited him as a wife. She was a good everyday woman, dependable, serviceable, comfortable, satisfying. She compared to Gilda as a good Chianti to Lacrima Christi, so to speak. As a wife, Gilda? No! But as a mistress! . . . He twisted his moustache, hummed, hawed in a satisfying way. Well, yes, undoubtedly, in a day or so. . . . Damn it, it was amusing. . . . Women!

He took her again to the opera, and to supper later. Something impelled him to speak of his other marriage, so called.

"You know, Gilda," he blurted out, "a word from you to the police and I should be rotting in a cell. Ugh! And good God! I should die! You had my life in your hands, Gilda, and you gave it back to me. You were always so good, Gilda, so noble, so kind!"

"I gave you my word," she said simply. "The word of a Coselschi."

Driving towards the Ritz, he attempted to take her in his arms.

"Aldo!" she protested, and held him away. "Remember! Queenie!"

"Damn Queenie!" he said nearly aloud. For the last few days, she had been surly, out of sorts, eyeing

A DAUGHTER OF THE MEDICI

him strangely, and mulling something over in her mind. Probably she was going to ask him to divorce Gilda and remarry herself in a legal manner. Of course she knew nothing of all this going on. How should she? She was getting difficult when he proposed going out in the evenings, on plea of business.

Again curse Queenie! For because of her Gilda would not submit to his hands or lips. . . .

In her apartment on Riverside Drive, amid the furniture of bastard Georgian design that had appeared so well in the Sixth Avenue department-store window, under the prints of the sportful Fragonard school that seemed so classy, as her term went, though somewhat free, Queenie Liverwright who called herself Marie Caracci, sat fuming, and there was malice in her Eastern eyes.

"So he thinks he'll get away with that stuff, hey? He thinks he can handle me that way, me that's done an' gone through so much for him!"

It was the third night running that Caracci had absented himself from her, had gone from the apartment on an ostensible business evening, "entertaining visiting bankers from the West." She knew whom he was entertaining. Well she knew!

A DAUGHTER OF THE MEDICI

"Only for me," she said to herself, "he'd be in jail. Yes, he would."

She had been a stenographer in the office of a downtown broker when he met and married her. He had taken her with his foreign ways and urgent courtship. Besides, he undoubtedly was going to be a very rich man. So her boss said. And her boss picked winners.

A battered copy of *Manhattan Gossip* was in her hand, and she pawed it over again until for the hundredth time under "Broadway Briefs" she re-read the paragraph that fascinated. "The secret of the identity of the Italian beauty who has been affecting the bright lights recently has at last been solved. She is Miss Gilda Coselschi, the daughter of the famous banking-house of Milan, as famous in Italy as Bertha Krupp in Germany. . . . Her companion is Giulio Caracci. . . ."

"I wasn't good enough to bring to the Florida Roof, hey? Not good enough to get my name in the paper?"

The sight of the paragraph shot her mind off at a tangent of personal vanity. Now that she lived on Riverside Drive, and had a smart roadster, she felt she could take an interest in the doings of society, and like many a thousand of her kind, studied it through the columns of the notorious weekly. She would have given many years of her life to be mentioned in its pages, even infamously.

She flared into sudden rage.

"I bet they're laughing at me up their sleeves," she stormed. "I ain't good enough to show around New York, but I was good enough to fool when he wanted a woman. I was a convenience, I was. They're playing me for a fool, are they? Hey? They're laughing at me——"

She reached for a telephone book, tearing its pages in her haste to get her number. "I'll show 'em," she snarled. "I'll show him who's the fool. I'll do him like he done me—dirt. Gi' me Spring 3100," she called into the telephone receiver. "Yeh, I said Spring 3100! Ain't ye got any ears? Spring 3100? That Police Headquarters? Listen! . . ."

Of all the evenings he had spent with Gilda, Aldo felt this was the crowning one. He had taken her to a noted roof garden after a visit to the theatre. About the tables waiters hovered unctuously in a manner that delighted his bourgeois heart. For him, Aldo Cesi, son of a laundress, these deft servitors were engaged. For him these star comedians and lovely girls disported themselves—to win his approval.

A DAUGHTER OF THE MEDICI

Opposite him the most beautiful woman in Italy sat, sick of love for him, he told himself.

She had never seemed more beautiful. Above her evening frock her warm shoulders shone like heavy silk, and her neck was white and flexible as a swan's. She was so aloof to the rest, he told himself, so loving to him, and yet her foolish scruples. . . . And, after all, wasn't she his wife?

"Listen, Gilda," he murmured warmly. "If you love me enough to forgive for what I had done in a moment of madness, thinking I had lost you forever, could you not love me a little now? You used not to be so cold, Gilda. There were times, I remember——"

She raised her face and, following her look, he saw that a burly, black-moustached man had drawn a chair up to the table.

"This table is engaged," Aldo snapped. "Oh, is that so?" The visitor regarded him with a sort of impudent contempt. "Your name is Caracci?" With a flick of thumb, like a juggler's trick, he showed an ominous silver badge attached to his vest. "You better come along," he said pleasantly. "The Captain wants to see you."

"What for?" The Italian's voice was thick.

A DAUGHTER OF THE MEDICI

"You know what for," the detective answered professionally.

Cesi raised his head to his wife's face. Gilda would save him, he felt in panic, she loved him so; she had always been so good to him. His jaw dropped suddenly, and his eyes dilated. A strange woman sat before him, and on her face was the hard, implacable, contemptuous look a doge of Venice's lady might have for the commoner who had insulted her. And about her mouth a smile quivered, and without a tremor her beautiful white slim hands lay before her, like resting butterflies.

II

CHAMPIONS

The noise of the great crowd in the arena without had taken on suddenly a new note. All evening, through the preliminary matches, the comments and applause had resembled the chattering of innumerable parrots, deepening occasionally at the climaxes of the fights into the muffled roar of light artillery. But now it had become vast and insistent, like the bourdon note on an organ, and it rumbled into the dressing-room like a powerful wind. The audience was demanding the star bout.

The little featherweight trainer glanced across at Regan's great bulk, sitting tensely on the couch. He looked at his watch. The seconds caught up their towels and half arose.

"Time to be getting in, Jim," the trainer warned.

But Regan didn't hear him. Neither did he hear the thunder of the crowd outside. So Big Dan was dead! Big Dan, the great champion! Big Dan, the biggest of them all! Regan had received the telegram an hour ago. Pneumonia, it said, and

CHAMPIONS

complications. As if pneumonia and complications could have killed Big Dan! He had died because he hadn't wanted to live, and because his heart was broken. That was the beginning and the end of it, if they wanted to know. And his heart was broken because he, the best and squarest of them all, the man who held his championship as a trust, had been beaten by this vaudeville favourite, this money-grubbing pan-handler whom he, Regan, was to fight to-night. That was what had killed Big Dan. Those were the complications that had aided pneumonia.

The audience had wearied of shouting and had now begun to stamp their feet. It sounded like the thudding of giants' hammers on some mighty anvil. Here and there could be distinguished faintly a shrill whistle, as the high note of fifes might be caught vaguely through the marching of a hundred thousand men.

Davy, the trainer, tapped Regan on the shoulder.

"Come on, lad," he urged. "They'll be tearing down the house inside of a minute."

Regan sprang up quickly and gathered his dressing-robe about him. "I'm coming," he said savagely.

Dave was worried. He took a long, shrewd glance at the set face of his boxer. Had Jim gone stale,

CHAMPIONS

he asked himself? The man was usually jolly before a fight, bantering the seconds, fooling with the promoter, making playful passes at Davy himself. And in the ring he was cool and level-headed, without a smile but without a frown, a great ring-general and a splendid boxer; but something was wrong with him to-night. His mouth was tight, and his nostrils twitched; his lips were closed to thin lines, and his powerful, lean jaws were shut like a vice.

"Take off that robe," the trainer commanded. "Let me take a look at you."

Regan swung the faded robe off and stood up, and Dave's heart jumped with pride, as it always did before a fight when he saw this man of his in fighting trim. Tall and powerful he stood up, in his green boxing-shorts, his black fighting-boots and the heavy adhesive tapes on his hands. Two hundred and seven pounds he had weighed in an hour ago; and he stood six feet and a half-inch tall. The trainer glanced proudly at the long, slim legs, at the fine waist and huge barrel of chest, at the arms like another man's thighs. There were no marks on him, either, except for the scar of the cut over the left eyebrow and the swelling of the left ear. Big Dan had done that in their three fights together. Splen-

CHAMPIONS

did! But Jim's face—Davy had never seen such a tense expression on it, had never seen such hardness in the grey eyes.

"He knows it," the trainer said to himself with a drooping of the heart. Regan knew he was going to be beaten to-night. In all Regan's thirteen years of boxing only one man had beaten him, and that had been Big Dan O'Connor, who had beaten him three times. Those defeats had been on points only, had not been by knock-outs. But to-night something different might happen. This New Zealander, who had knocked out Big Dan, might he not drop Regan as he had dropped the great champion, an inert and pitiable thing huddled on the canvas?

"I wish we hadn't taken it on," the trainer muttered.

"Come on," Regan snapped. He pulled the robe about him again. "I'm all right."

They swung out of the room and down the corridor. The seconds led the way with their buckets and towels. The torrent of sound in the arena rose to the dimensions of a cataract. Forward, past a black sea of coats crowned by a foam of heads, the ring rose, square and roped, ghastlily blue under the cluster of arc-lamps, sputtering violet flame

CHAMPIONS

like some captured star. In a corner of the ring the white-shirted referee lolled, indifferent to all the clamour about him. Somebody clambered into the ring and threw four brown gloves on the floor.

As he crawled through the ropes and sat down in his corner, careless of the shouts of greeting to him from the audience, the old, seemingly eternal grind began in his head. So Big Dan was gone, and gone not three hours ago, at that! There was no doubt about it. The defeat had killed him. Regan had been at the ringside when it happened, in Dan's corner; and he, with all the house, had looked aghast while Davies' snakelike left hand pecked and pecked and pecked at the old fighter's eyes until he had been blinded. Davies had run away, snapping and biting with his left, until Dan was dazed and worn out. Time and again either of Dan's arms would lash out, and the New Zealander would roll away from the punch by some marvel of acrobacy.

Davies called his method of fighting ring-craft, but he never acted as though he were in a ring, fighting for an immense thing like the championship of the world. He seemed to be some crafty schemer, planning to capture something that meant money. The New Zealander could hit like a trip-hammer,

CHAMPIONS

but he never took a chance. He had depended on his ring-craft and generalship to win, he told the public. Ring-craft? The cunning of a peddler! Generalship? The tactics of a tight-rope-walker!

And even the knockout of Dan, that hadn't been clean. Davies, blinded and jarred as his opponent was, hadn't the nerve to feint and jump in and shoot the right over. He was still afraid of Dan's terrific uppercuts. Suddenly Dan's manager shouted a piece of advice in the twelfth round. The old battler—dazed or he would never have done it—turned his head around to his corner and half lowered his guard. At that moment the New Zealander had sneaked his right home to the jaw, stealthily, craftily, like a thug of the streets black-jacking a man from behind.

"Here he comes," the trainer announced, as he moistened his dry lips.

A great cheer swept through the hall. It rose in a wild pæan of frenzy and reverberated among the rafters and swung through the chinks and crevices of the door and window to the mob outside. The telegraph-instruments began to chatter like castanets. Regan turned about on his chair and cursed at them savagely. So they used to cheer for Big Dan!

CHAMPIONS

The champion vaulted over the ropes into the ring. A platoon of seconds followed him, resplendent in white sweaters. Davies stood for a moment acknowledging their applause. His manager threw a big scarlet robe about him, and he sat down. The cheering still crashed like thunder.

"Listen to them, Dave!" Regan laughed harshly at the trainer. "Listen to them!"

A great nausea against the cheering multitude seized Regan. They cheered for Big Dan; that was right. Big Dan had always impressed them with the greatness of the game. When the old champion had fought, the great, elemental, eternal struggle of the universe had been driven home to them, and the giant boxer had seemed the type of skilful, forceful human being who, by either brain or brawn, triumphed in battle and rose supreme. But Big Dan was gone now, and was forgotten, and another reigned in his stead, a shoddy pinchbeck king. It was like the fickleness of the tribe in the desert that had forgotten the prophet who led them straightly through peril and oppression, and when he disappeared among the lightnings and thunder of Sinai, had at once fallen prone before a gilded calf.

The announcer was bawling like a megaphone.

". . . the heavyweight championship of the

CHAMPIONS

world between Ben Davies, the Kangaroo of New Zealand, the champion, conqueror of Tom McCormack of Ireland; of Bandsman Benson, England's best; of Cyclone Johnny Wills, the Australian; of Big Dan O'Connor, of America, . . . and Jim Regan, the Pride of Sheepshead Bay. . . . twenty rounds to a decision."

A hush fell on the audience for an instant; then the noise began again, though subdued into a light susurrus of conversation that seemed no more than the soughing of a faint wind. The voices of the attendants showing late comers to their seats could be heard distinctly above the chatter—that and the melancholy cries of the boys peddling programmes and lemonade. Blue smoke from the cigars and cigarettes hovered about the ring in hazy whorls and arabesques, assuming grotesque shapes like the shapes of clouds.

The champion crossed the ring to shake hands.

"I don't want that," Regan snapped. "Here, show me your bandages." He caught at the hands, examined and dropped them. The champion walked back, smiling contemptuously.

Regan looked at the crowd again with an expression of bitterness. Not content with Big Dan, they wanted another victim. They wanted to see again

CHAMPIONS

this new idol of theirs knock out another of those old-timers who were supposed to be invincible. Well, just let them see it!

"Believe me, you'll see something," Regan muttered through his clenched teeth.

He would be beaten; he was sure of that. Knocked out too, the first time in his life; if the man could do that to Big Dan, he could also do it to the lesser man of his time. But before that would happen, they would see a fight that would go down in their memories, in their fickle, evanescent memories, for years to come. For to-night he was not going to fight his own battle, but the battle of the dead man in Arizona, for whom the immortal gong had just sounded, and who was climbing into the ring of the Greatest and Cleanest Sportsman of them all, where no foul blows were countenanced and no unfair counts permitted, and all had the same square deal, the oldest of the battered champions and the youngest of challengers.

The referee called them to the centre for instructions. Impatiently Regan listened to the familiar warnings against holding and hitting in clinches, against wrestling or roughing, against the pivot-punch. He strode back to his corner. The seconds deserted the ring. He rubbed his shoes on the resin-

CHAMPIONS

board, and took one heft at the ropes. The gong crashed out in a shivering, brazen note. Regan turned about and strode to the centre of the ring.

The audience sat straight in their seats and held their breaths for an instant. Under the greenish glare of the arc-lights they could see the two contestants like a photograph of statuary. There was the champion, symmetrical, lithe, pink and fresh-looking, his guard loose and well up to his high-coloured, heavy-jawed face, with the glare overhead turning his reddish hair to white. There was Regan, heavy about the neck and shoulders, slim in the waist, slight in the legs, his long black head and lean jaw cuddled into his shoulder, his left arm out at full length, his right drawn like a bowstring. The four brown gloves flickered in the air like the paws of cats. Their feet shuffled sibilantly on the canvas. The boards creaked whiningly beneath their feet as they moved.

How long would it last, the onlookers asked themselves with titillating, nervous interest. How long would Davies let him go before he put away this last of the old school of fighters? Of course it was easy for the champion. These old fellows hadn't the science of the new school; they knew only how to fight, not to box. Regan was a dangerous man to the ordinary ring-men, with his crashing left lead and terrific follow-up with the right, but against this new wonder, who knew boxing as a physician knows medicine, what chance had he? At any rate, it would be a fight to remember, the old school against the new. They hoped Regan would last as long as the old champion had lasted. There was not much chance, though!

The men were moving faster as they sparred. Their gloves cut the air in quick, stilted movements, like the jerking actions of marionettes; and as they swung around, the audience noticed that in contrast to the champion's superior and slightly contemptuous smile, Regan's face was drawn into something that resembled a snarl; his eyes had a bitter, bright reflection such as might be in the eyes of a hunting leopard stalking a deer—a glance that made them somehow uneasy, as though it were directed against themselves in place of against the blonde giant in the ring.

There was a quick lead from Davies to the jaw that Regan flicked aside with his right glove—then a smashing right swing that he slipped inside of, a moment's futile driving in the clinch, the referee's staccato order to break away.

CHAMPIONS

An instant's quick spar, and Regan's left hand flashed out in a vicious hook. The champion slipped back. Regan's right followed up like a thunderbolt. It missed by an inch. The audience smiled. Regan was getting the lesson Big Dan got, that smashing hooks are avoided easily, and that rights can be sidestepped. And as they smiled, Regan's arm whipped over a second left swing that cracked home with a snap as of wood breaking. His right hand smashed home like a piston to the body. A mad clinch for an instant, and Regan wrenched himself loose and tore in an uppercut that thudded like a mallet on wood. Blindly they saw the champion holding on in frenzy.

"Break away! Break!" came the voice of the referee, full and commanding.

The gong boomed out sullenly the end of the round.

As Regan sat in his corner between the rounds, the cold sponge slipping over his chest and the towels about him cracking like gunshots, he slapped one gloved hand into the other wrathfully; his teeth clicked; his feet beat a tattoo on the floor.

"Don't get excited, Jim," a second whispered.

"Leave him be!" Dave the trainer ordered.

CHAMPIONS

Regan had heard, as he wrestled in Davies' corner in that first futile clinch, the overdressed, supercilious, under-sized manager of the champion discussing the bout with the promoter.

"Davies could put him out in the first," the promoter had sneered.

"Sure he could," the champion's manager had lisped back. He shook his head in agreement until his pince-nez wobbled. His hands went out in expostulation. "But we got to think of the movies, Mr. Swartz. We got to think of the movies. Ben will fake through until the twelfth. Then—good night!"

That was what had called forth Regan's smashing attack. Fake the fight until the twelfth round, for the sake of the money those purring machines on the platform would bring in, money extracted from the public dishonestly, on the plea that this was a straight fight! Was it straight, if a fellow could knock another out in the first, that he should stall through until the twelfth? It wasn't honest, and what was worse, it wasn't sport. Lord! He remembered the third fight of Big Dan and himself, who were the best of friends. They had met in the street during training, and Dan had called to him.

CHAMPIONS

"How's the training, Jim?" the champion had asked.

"Fine, Dan!" Regan answered. "I'm going to take that championship away from you."

"My son, you've got a fat chance!" Dan had laughed. "I'm planning to put you asleep."

"At any rate," Regan predicted, "it's going to be a good fight."

And it had been a good fight, from the first round until the last, and they had both fought mercilessly. They had fought for the good of the sport and the honour of the game. There was no faking there!

The gong rang its brazen summons for the second round, and he stepped forward carelessly. Something stung him on the right jaw, stung him again, shifted its attack to his temple. It was the champion's left hand trying to wear him down with the tactics that had dazed and blinded Dan. He laughed savagely and rushed in, swinging both hands viciously. Davies flitted away. The audience laughed. Regan gritted his teeth together and stood back. Again the left hand pecked him.

"I'll get home a few on you," he said to himself. "Before they carry me out, I'll leave my mark on you."

CHAMPIONS

A queer, cold feeling came over him, a calm, white rage, that here was something before him—this flitting, pecking figure—with which he must get into close and mortal combat. He would go down himself, but before he went down he must inflict enduring wounds on it. It was as though that dead, inert man lying pitifully stiff some thousands of miles away was calling on him, as the nearest thing to him, weak though the instrument was, to wreak some measure of vengeance on the agency of his ruin. It might have been some dead king, murdered by stealth, whose blood called out to a kinsman for punishment on the usurper.

Regan moved about the ring carefully, calculatingly, using every ounce of his old ring-craft to the best advantage, for he knew that to get his opening he must use every stratagem at his command. Once he had it, then he could let that Berserker rage pent up in him burst forth, and put every muscle in his powerful frame into crushing, stinging blows—the blows Big Dan should have inflicted, had he ever got the chance.

A few light leads to the head and body ducked and stopped; a short rapid spar—and the champion's hand shot out straight for the jaw. Regan was amazed at the ease with which he knocked it aside

CHAMPIONS

with his right. His massive left arm shot out like a trip-hammer. Only the roll of the champion's head saved him from a knockdown. An uppercut jarred on Regan's chin as he jumped in, but it only woke the challenger up. In a blind fury he ripped both hands to the body, alternating with crushing upward hooks to the jaw.

"The bell, man!" the referee tore at his arms. "The bell!" The round was over.

He did not notice, so much was he blinded within himself by this terrible, passionate rage, the wild clatter of the telegraph-keys or the hush in the body of the hall. He did not lean back with his arms on the ropes gasping in the air. He sat rigid in his chair, one hand on his knee, and his muscles tensed, glaring into an empty space. Mechanically he rinsed his throat with the water they gave him—submitted to the lemon between his lips.

"Money!" he snarled suddenly. "Money!"

"What's wrong, Jim?" an advising second asked in panic. "What is it?"

"Leave him be," the trainer demanded. "Do you hear me, you? Leave him be!"

Money! Had ever Big Dan counted a house before he decided whether he should fight hard or stall? Had ever Big Dan gone on the vaudeville

CHAMPIONS

stage, sandwiched between a woman dancer and a made-up man singer of mushy songs? Had ever Big Dan postured in a ring so that a cinematograph could catch his huge triceps and powerful chest? Regan remembered the occasion when Sandy Anderson was to fight Cyclone Maher: Anderson fell ill, lost his forfeit, lost the bout—and the man wanted the money so badly—something about trouble his father had got into, with a mortgage. Big Dan had heard of it.

"That's all right," he had said in an offhand way. "We must stick together. I've got none myself just now; but I'll fight anybody they get for me, and the kid can have my end."

And he had. Big Dan had fought, thirteen gruelling rounds with Sailor Jones. Anderson was dead when the bout was over, but there was enough in Dan's end to fix up the trouble in the dead boxer's family, to pay for the funeral and to put Sandy's wife and child outside the danger of want.

There had been also the time when Dan had been matched to fight Carl Sellers, the giant negro who was called "The Cotton-hook," so terrible was his right-hand punch. The greatest purse in ring history had been offered, and a special arena was built for the fight. Then came the trouble with

CHAMPIONS

Spain, and Dan slipped out of his training quarters quietly and came back within an hour. A telephone-call got the promoter down from New York hot-foot.

"I'm sorry, Paddy," Dan had told the promoter. "The fight's off. I'm away to-morrow to Cuba or Porto Rico, or somewhere like that, toting a gun."

The Irish promoter shook him by the hand.

"Good man!" he had said. That was all. He understood. Even the Cotton-hook understood, and had no rancour, only admiration. Those were the days when boxers were men, not adding-machines! And Dan, the mighty one, the hero of a hundred battles, the clean, the straight, the honourable—Dan was dead.

It seemed to Regan, as he stood out there under a flare of electricity, with the springing boards beneath his feet, with the ropes about him, that he and this other fighter were alone in the world. Forgotten were the white faces of the audience, blanched to the hue of lime—the purring cameras, the raucous warnings of the referee. Mechanically he jabbed and led, slipped from hook and uppercut, rolled to the heavy swings to his head. Mechanically his left shot out like a piston, and his right swung in with a crash. Mechanically he crossed and hooked, ripped home uppercut after uppercut, drove his right to the kidneys in the clinches or upwards to the base of the skull. He might have been on a mountain-top lonely and dark, with the wind howling about him, and he fighting and struggling with this man, and the only witness to it the stiffened figure whose death and defeat he was striving to avenge.

He strode back to his corner at the end of the sixth round and sat bolt upright in his chair. Above the crack of the towels and the clicking telegraph he caught the voice of one second to another.

"Davies' wind's gone," he said, "and they're massaging his legs."

Regan laughed again to himself. Of course the man wasn't in condition! The only reason he would ever get into condition was that there was money to make, and to make it a man had to train. He never felt the elation of a springy body from heel to head, the glory in rippling muscles and perfect health, the sense of power, the keen brain that thought out the action, and the hand that performed it. It was hard to get him to train, the papers said. Big Dan had never been out of condition. He never hung about pothouses, telling people what a great fighter he was, accepting the adulation of sycophant and parasite. When Dan wasn't fighting, he was

CHAMPIONS

out on his big ranch, talking to his people, playing with his kids. . . .

"Time!" the trainer warned. He whipped the stool from under Regan. The bell clanged.

A rushing hurricane of blows struck him as he stood up. The champion had sprung from his corner and was tearing into him with the mad ferocity of a panther. Regan's guard was beaten down. He was buffeted about the head as by giant waves. An uppercut crashed home beneath his heart with the force of a shell. He felt Davies' right strike his jaw like a piledriver. For an instant the ring heeled like a boat in a sea-way. The flaring lamps went out into darkness. He felt somehow as though he had been swung over a precipice into the void beneath the world. In his ears there was a singing, as of brown bees.

Body and mind came together suddenly. By some supreme effort of will Regan called himself back to consciousness and began fighting blindly. The challenger had stood back to let him drop, after that terrible hook to the jaw, the hook that had dropped Big Dan!

"He's gone," one of Davies' seconds shouted in exultation. "He's done for now."

Regan's left hand struck back to the jaw like the

crack of a whip. His right thudded home to the ribs. He swept Davies across the ring with a storm of hooks and smashes that had the force of a stinging gale. The champion covered up. He withdrew his head behind his arms, as a turtle would draw its head within its carapace. Regan stepped back. The crowd hooted suddenly.

"Fight him, Ben," Regan heard from the ringside. "You big coward! He's beating you."

As they sparred around, Regan caught a glimpse of a woman who had the sharp-pointed face of a fox. Her teeth were drawn and snarling. Her black hair was bound closely about by a fillet of brilliants. She was in evening dress, with a red satin operacloak about her shoulders. And in her eyes was all the evil in the world.

Regan knew who it was. She was the famous dancer from the Folies Bergère whom Davies had married in Paris. He had seen her portrait in the papers, and had read accounts of her extravagances and escapades—the last of which was to marry the heavyweight champion of the world.

"Go after him, Ben," she was shouting. "Knock the old stiff out."

A great sense of immodesty suffused Regan at the thought of this woman's being here and directing

CHAMPIONS

her husband from the ringside—yes, and taunting him! He knew nothing of women—except one, and she had been dead these dozen years. But he knew the wife of Big Dan, that powerful, brown-faced Irish woman with the placid manner and the trustful grey eyes. She lived for nothing except her husband and her children. She had a soft place in her big heart for Regan, because he seemed so alone in the world and because he was a friend of Dan's. She would never have sat at a ringside as this shameless hussy was doing. Regan remembered how she used to come to the city where Dan was fighting. She would stay in a sitting-room in the nearest hotel until the battle was over.

"Good-bye, missis," Dan would say as he left, and the great paw that could have felled an ox would descend on her shoulder as lightly as gossamer.

"Good-bye, Dan," she would answer placidly, and then huskily beneath her breath would come the "God bless you!"

Dan never knew what she did while he was fighting; neither did the world—only Regan. And she had told it to him simply because he loved Dan too. She used to kneel in that cold hotel room, telling her beads over and over.

CHAMPIONS

Only once had Regan seen her moved. That was the night Dan had come home after losing the championship. He had come back still unsteady from that crash on the jaw. His face had been cut and swollen and puffed from that pecking left. She had rushed to him.

"Oh, my God!" she had cried in terror.

"It's all right, missis." Dan had attempted to smile. She had looked at the battered face of the champion. Her eyes had suddenly snapped fire, and her breast heaved. Her hands had clenched like vices.

"Who did this?" she had demanded. "Jim Regan, tell me, who did this to my man?"

They had turned away shamefaced, manager, trainer and seconds. They could not stand up before the passion in her face.

"I'll kill him," she had said savagely. "I'll find him out and kill him with my own bare hands." It had taken hours to pacify her.

And she was sitting there to-night by the side of her dead husband, she who had been as big a woman as Big Dan had been a man. She knew, as well as Regan knew, what had killed the old champion. To-morrow morning she would read in the papers of Davies' next fight. She would read that Dan's best friend had gone down before the champion

CHAMPIONS

as Dan had gone down. But she would read that the end had come only after a terrific battle, a battle in which the champion had received blows whose mark he would bear until his dying day. And she would know that Regan hadn't fought his own fight throughout it. She would know whence had come the vigour and the stunning violence of the blows. She would know what fury had actuated him. Yes, she would understand. . . .

"Mind that right, Jim," a second advised.

"Can't you leave him be?" Dave the trainer raved. "For God's sake, can't you leave him be?"

"Tenth round, son," he whispered. The seconds sprang out through the ropes. The gong boomed brazenly, like the stroke of a church bell.

For many rounds now the audience had sat back breathless and somewhat aghast. Time and again the bell clanged out its harsh demand. The number of rounds flickered and twinkled in the electric indicator overhead. They paid no attention to these things. During the round they were breathless and tense, during the intermission limp and worn. The hoarse buzz of conversation had ceased, and even the attendants stood frozen in their places.

For these men felt they were watching something epochal, something epic. They had come there to

CHAMPIONS

see the champion of champions toy with a sparring partner for a few rounds, to see him exhibit his wonderful defensive science and then to see his right hand flash out like a snake's fang and the victim roll over face downward. That was all they expected.

And instead of that they had seen a huge figure, tense in the mouth, blazing of eyes, half whalebone and half steel, it seemed, outbox, outfeint, outfight the man who had been heralded to them as the master craftsman of them all. They saw this huge figure, pick off blows in the air as a juggler picks off balls; they saw him glide like a ghost away from blows that whirred through the air like a flail.

They saw Regan's left snap home like a whip, and his right rip in like a battering-ram. They saw him use all the old forgotten ring-craft—the sparring into position until time and distance were calculated to a hairbreadth; the marvellous movement of feet where not a single ounce of energy was wasted; the working of his opponent into a corner or against the ropes with the certainty and caution of a cat stalking a mouse.

And what was more than that, they saw Regan take a blow that would have felled an ox, flush on the jaw, and then fight back like an unchained fury. They were no longer looking at Jim Regan, it seemed.

CHAMPIONS

They were looking at some terrible supernatural figure, descended from the misty top of Olympus, where he had been boxer to some pagan god—at the shade of one of the old Roman fighters who wielded the terrible iron cestus.

Davies was gone, they could see. They saw the champion, whom they had come to applaud, grow weaker and more tired round after round. They saw, with a vague sense of pity, the battered sides and sagging jaw, the uncertain feet, the drooping knees. They saw him cover up and cringe back, as a coward might under the lash of the whip. They ceased being contemptuous of him. They were only pitiful—and afraid.

They had come to applaud the champion. They had come in, well-fed, comfortable, seeking an evening's amusement. They wanted to see Davies in action, as they phrased it. And as the battle went on, and the tide turned, they wanted to show their appreciation of this other man, this fighting fury, terrible as an army with banners. They raised their hands to applaud and opened their throats to shout, but it came home to them with a grisly feeling along the spine that this was something bigger than a bout between hired fighters, something fearsomely elemental, like the eternal conflict between thunder and lightning and earth and sea. They shivered as they sat there; their hands remained apart; their throats refused their office; the hand-claps wavered, and the cheering died.

"Twelfth round!" the trainer whispered. The gong clanged.

Regan's head was dizzy as he went forward to the ring-centre, from that trip-hammer hook in the tenth. Another of those would finish him, he knew. He had been fifteen years boxing now, and for years there had not been the sting to his punches that there had been when he was in his prime. Only a straight, clean existence kept him his position in the ring—that and his eternally good condition; but his hands didn't respond to his brain as they used to, and he had not the same easy movement of shoulder and arm. Another punch like that, and he was done!

"He'll get me sure, this round," he muttered.

To be sure, Davies would get him, get him in the same round as he got Big Dan. In a few minutes they would carry him out, cheering the champion, as they had cheered him the night Dan went out. But before that happened, Regan swore, he would strike one more punch. He was the last of the old ringmen, of the line that Cribb was of, and Molyneaux the black man, and Bendigo, and the Benicia

CHAMPIONS

Boy—the men who had been men and fighters and sportsmen, who had been the friends of nobles, who had stood before kings. For them he would strike one more blow. For them and for their companion man-at-arms! For Big Dan!

The referee was hovering about like a small, excited bird. His feet pattered strangely on the canvas, like a dog's pads. Very carefully Regan dropped into crouching attitude. Carefully he sparred his man toward the ropes. His hands flickered as they feinted and cut. The champion retreated uneasily.

"He's saving himself," Regan thought; "he's saving himself to finish me."

The champion was near the ropes now, shifting his guard with every feint. Regan settled himself, and fiddled with his left hand. He feinted the right suddenly, as though he were going to cross it to the head. The champion's guard went up. Regan drew back his left, as though he were going to volley it to the plexus. The champion's hands dropped. With a grunt, Regan shifted his feet, and spinning around in mid-air, his right hand smashed home, full and flush to the jaw, as true as a poleaxe to the head of a beeve.

He stumbled over something as he tried to regain his balance, and he caught on to the ropes to keep

CHAMPIONS

straight. He was dizzy now, and blown from the effort, and he hung on there swaying, looking blindly at the house. A great hush seemed to have come over it. Somewhere he could hear a voice faintly:

". . . three—four—five. . . ."

He swung about, his guard up. The referee was standing over Davies. The champion was lying on the canvas, face downward. The referee's arm was going up and down, in easy, swinging gestures, like a musician conducting an orchestra.

". . . eight—nine. . . ."

Regan's head was clearing. The scene took form and meaning before his eyes. Davies was out. The punch for Big Dan had gone home! The punch for Big Dan! The punch for Big Dan!

". . . ten. Out!"

He stood still, his hands on his hips, watching the seconds as they carried the champion to his corner. He felt a great, clean sense of elation sweep through him, like a sea-wind. Something had been done that should have been done. Words choked him. Coherent thought would not come.

A vast, explosive torrent of sound struck on his eardrums—a tearing, raucous cry, as of a great crowd in hysteria. It screamed like the notes of a gigantic bagpipe, a high-pitched crying against the

CHAMPIONS

background of a titanic drone. Dimly he knew that the little trainer was holding on to his gloved hand.

"Do you hear the cheers, Jimmy?" he was nearly sobbing. "Do you hear them cheer? You're champion of the world."

Thought came into his head at last, clear-cut, sibilant. He stepped forward and raised his hand.

"Quits for you, Dan!" he shouted. His voice rang out in a great passion of victory. Somehow he felt that his words would travel winged across mountain-top and valley and creep into the room where the dead man lay, surrounded by yellow candles, with his brown-faced, brooding wife at his head.

"You're champion, Jim," the trainer was repeating hysterically. "Don't you hear them cheer?"

He looked over the ropes at the maddened, cheering mob. Yes, they were cheering for him. They had cheered for Big Dan! They had cheered for the beaten thing in the corner! And now they were cheering for him! A sort of nausea filled him.

"You can keep your championship," he laughed. "I'm through!"

He leaped over the ropes lightly and strode to his dressing-room, through the lines of the frenzied thousands, oblivious of them, contemptuous of them, looking neither to the right nor left.

III

A HAPPY ENDING

About the farm-house there is the air of subdued tragedy. The Jersey cows in the ten-acre pasture field are troubled. They raise their heads. They low strangely. The little cocker spaniel hurries to and fro about the vine-clad porch, whining pathetically. He is looking for someone. But she is gone. Even her scent is gone.

If you hurry through the orchard to the knoll where that great drift of dogwood is, you can glimpse the little funeral procession on its way to the old resting ground; a hearse with two grey horses going slowly along the road of trees, and the broken procession following it in sombre black, showing against the white of the road like some strange formation of black ants. There she is, for whom the gentle cows are lowing, and whom the cocker spaniel seeks, with its whine like the pathetic cry of a small child.

May is abroad. The trees have burst into a piping green, and there is dogwood everywhere and apple-blossoms, and here and there violets and daffodils.

A HAPPY ENDING

Not infrequently a white-scutted rabbit scampers through the woods. The quick wind of approaching summer whips the trout streams and bellies the sails of the schooners forging out to sea.

A pathetic day for a young girl's burial! And some Gael seeing her home mutters, "Happy is the corpse whom the rain falls on," as though a spirit were not happier in the high perfumed air than clogged in the indefinite, opaque dew.

She is only twenty and she is dead. And her friends would say, "What a tragedy!" were they not a religious folk, not daring to question the supreme will of their God.

He wanted her to Himself, they tell themselves in an attempt to find solace for their sad hearts.

They shake their heads. The designs of Providence, they quote, are inscrutable.

Are they? After all one asks, are they?

She entered and moved across the café floor to an empty seat at an unoccupied table. The orchestra of three, not proven, Hawaiians followed her with their glance, as all the café did, the habitués because they couldn't quite place her, the occasional visitors because she was, in her hard brilliant way, beautiful.

A HAPPY ENDING

She threw her fur wrap from her shoulder, and gave a rapid order to a waiter. When she turned to look about the room, all saw that splendid aquiline head, groomed like a mare's coat, eyes clear and glistening, colour cunningly applied, hair waved as though it were an advertisement in some smart magazine, eyebrows trimmed and glossy, teeth polished like a precious stone.

"Some society dame who got the wrong steer," the occasionals voted her.

An instant later they saw her toss off neat spirits following it with a cunning chaser, then light a cigarette and draw the smoke deep into her lungs and emit it with a slow, thin exhalation.

"There's some tough baby, we'll say!" And the occasionals felt they had solved the problem.

But the habitués had not. And to be a puzzle to the habitués at the Palisades Club was in the nature of an achievement. The Palisades Club would imply, by its name alone, a company of quiet people addicted to nature. One might think of them as interested in the scenery of the Hudson. One could imagine them tramping the woods on Sunday in search of rare flowers. It would not be surprising to learn that they studied the habits of wild birds.

In reality the Palisades Club is, in the phrase

A HAPPY ENDING

of those who affect it, "the toughest joint this side of hell." It's quiet, of course. Certain police, with an itching palm and a great respect for outward seemliness, see to it that Herman—as its proprietor is called by his cronies and the police—"don't pull anything too raw." At two o'clock of a Sunday morning it is at its best for dancing, "spielers" and "sharp-shooters" dancing to the strains of the negroid orchestra. Folks who consider the "shimmy" objectionable in the Coney Island version should see it at the Palisades Club. At Coney they have seen merely a pale imitation.

Sleigh-riders, or users of cocaine, can obtain all they desire there. The cocaine privilege is held by an adroit youth whose name, if I remember rightly, is Yaphank Harry. Up a discreet flight of stairs, across the leads of a roof, to the window of a near-by tenement is the road to the Hongkong Club, where the peanut-oil lamp is lighted night and day and opium smokers lie, their heads on one another's hips, dreaming forty years of life away in two rapid years.

The women who come to the Palisades Club are of two sorts. One is the woman who can be hired, the others have their photographs with great regularity in the Sunday supplements. They are actresses

A HAPPY ENDING

from musical comedies who have married rich men, captains of finance or legatees of hereditary wealth, and who have risen from the lowest social level. Time and again these women have been afflicted with a terrible *nostalgie de la boue*, or a homesickness for the gutter, and they have come to revel a night in the Palisades Club and then to return for a lengthy period to their life of recently acquired inhibitions.

But Blondie, as they called the habitual uncatalogued woman, was neither of them. She drank with gusto, but never past certain limits. She danced with sundry who asked her. It was all because she liked to do it—because she had acquired a taste for this life. Somewhere nearby—on the Drive, most likely—she had an apartment whose expenses were paid by a capitalist downtown. The venal women there considered her very lucky.

"She's living the life of Reilly," they said in envy, "and she's got a grip on herself."

The second thing was the important thing. When one is hanging on the edge of a social precipice, a firm grip is a splendid thing. But sooner or later even the firmest of fingers must weaken, and there is an abyss below.

At times Blondie's eyes would grow tremendously bitter, as she sat there with her drink and cigarette.

A HAPPY ENDING

She liked these things, and she hated herself for liking them. All the Palisades Club-fellows knew that look—it came on one when crowded by the ghosts of what might have been. Most of them in that mood dispelled it with a deck of snow bought from Yaphank Harry, or walked the tiles to the Hongkong Club to smoke a few pills of opium. But Blondie dispelled it with an effort alone. A fine girl, Blondie! Yes, a fine girl!"

The eyes of the Club left Blondie for new entrants at the door—a man with a fur coat, in evening clothes, and two women of the upper world. The Club breathed excitedly. If there was anything it loved it was a slumming party. There was a certainty always of picking a pocketbook, or a necklace, or other jewellery, even of a hold-up outside—for the victims would never make a complaint, else they would have to explain what they were doing in the most notorious dive in the city.

But they turned with a snarl from the massaged, brilliantly groomed leader of the party.

"Hell!" they swore. "It's Tony Van Stetter."

And to touch Van Stetter was one of the few things the police would not allow. The holder of the Van Stetter millions was no sap to be trimmed. His bank

A HAPPY ENDING

was the invisible executive offices of three-fourths of the nation's commerce. His grip was at the throat of municipal things. Anyone who troubled Van Stetter would be "got." That was enough.

The Club had turned away in disappointment, but it swivelled around again to the group, for suddenly there was a tenseness in the air. Blondie had risen from her table, and had come across to where Van Stetter was standing.

"Marcelle!" they heard him call her.

"Tony!" Her smile was bitter.

"What are you doing here?"

"Isn't this the place for me?"

"Humph!" He turned aside. She touched him on the arm. He swung around.

"What do you want with me?"

His tone was ugly. It was no part of the slumming programme to be faced with a woman of the underworld in front of his Madison Avenue friends.

"Just this, Tony."

She must have had the little automatic in her hand as she rose from the table, for she immediately dotted his shirt-front with small black punctures, while the noise it made was like that of a wickedly cracking whip. At the second shot he went down but at each

A HAPPY ENDING

consecutive one he attempted to rise. At the eighth he lay still. He was dead.

Then things happened as in a badly directed moving-picture, all huddled, all hurried, with no values of dramatic timing. Suddenly police were there, and a plain-clothes man with the face and build of a crapulous bar keeper was manacling her wrists and regarding her with hot, savage eyes.

"You know who you croaked, hey? You know who you croaked?"

"Yes," Blondie told him.

"You croaked Mr. Van Stetter. And you know what you're going to get for it, hey? You're going to get the chair. Make me? The chair!"

"I know." Blondie seemed quite satisfied.

"She sure put this place on the bum, Blondie did," the habitués grumbled. "We got to get a new hangout, and we won't get that for a while. But did you make her when that big bum pinched her? They're going to burn her for this"—as their stark locution for the chair goes. "And she knows it. But did she flap an eye? Did she? We'll say she didn't. She's one game jane, that's what she is, Blondie is. . . ."

She had known for a week now that Van Stetter was trying to engineer a row that would separate

63

A HAPPY ENDING

them definitely. To-night she felt the occasion had come. It was nearing one o'clock in the morning and her guests had been scattered by his sudden appearance as a flock of birds is scattered by the sound of a shot. She waited for him to speak.

He avoided looking at her. His eye roved about the room—at the scattered cards on the table; at the cigarette ends piled up on the nouveau-art ash-trays; at the half-empty siphons and decanters placed here and there. He hadn't taken off his light overcoat, and he still held his gloves and hat and stick. He had dropped in, he said, on his way home from his club.

"I thought I told you, Marcelle, those people weren't good for you."

"I know nobody else," she told him calmly. She looked at him for an instant. "Do you think it easy for"—she paused for an instant and then hit him straight between the eyes—"for a kept woman to make friends of whom you would approve."

"There is no necessity for crowding your apartment with the scum of Broadway. If you had gone out to pick the most disreputable acquaintances in New York, you couldn't have done the job more efficiently."

"They have been kind to me," she said with dignity. "They cannot be as bad as you say."

A HAPPY ENDING

"As bad as I say! As bad! Don't you know how Benton Bassett makes his money?"

"A playwright."

"He's the most finished blackmailer in America. His friend Lonzer is a cocaine addict and a professional card sharp. Your friend Mamie Hedges has a police-court record in three cities, and Olive Ryan was connected with a disreputable murder in Cincinnati. Now can you tell me those are proper acquaintances for you?" He lent point to his speech with a scowl.

"I'll tell you one thing, Tony: these folk have been honest with me, and that's more than you have."

"You know what will happen if you go ahead with them," he observed casually and with a certain pleasure in his voice. "In six months you will be in the gutter. In a year you will be dead."

"You have seen it happen before, haven't you, Tony?" Her voice was smooth as satin, but there was a dreadful unheard acerbity in it. "To women; to women friends of yours; to women you said you loved; to women to whom you gave every luxury. Haven't you, Tony?"

He flushed a little. She had penetrated his inner consciousness.

"It comes to this—either they go or I do."

"It may surprise you to hear that they don't go."

A HAPPY ENDING

"Then I do." He pulled on his gloves, and turned to the door.

"Understand me," he said, "when I go now, I don't come back."

"I understand you, Tony," she replied meaningly. "I understand you too well. I couldn't understand you better. Good-bye! Close the door as you go."

When he had gone she stood trembling for an instant, and then, sinking into the nearest chair, she broke into harsh, terrible crying. And then a gust of hysterical laughter broke from her in rapid, defined flows. She stood up then and wiped her eyes, and there was a hard, defiant look on her face.

Well, she had been into the game and she had to play it. She had traded in her assets for multi-coloured seductive chips. She had discarded from the hand that had been dealt her. Now it was up to her to draw. What were the new cards likely to be?

Let us see. A half-dozen had tried to get her away from Van Stetter. There was Holstein, the shrewd Oriental of the department-store ring—a great business strategist who looked like a caricature in some anti-Semitic sheet. There was Badaurian, the Armenian, the premier rug importer, a strange

A HAPPY ENDING

being with the cunning of the devil himself and the hands of an awkward girl. There were Beltz the brewer, and others. Whom would she choose?

It was not a matter of personal predilection, she remembered. It was a game and a business. These Orientals, it came in a flash to her, were crazy for blonde women.

Let it be Badaurian!

She called the telephone operator.

"Central," she directed, "I want to get a number in Larchmont. . . . Yes, I said Larchmont."

She stepped out of the elevator in the bijou apartment house and followed him to the white door of the front apartment. At every step she made, she felt that her knees might collapse. At every breath she took she felt her heart could no longer stand the terrific pounding. She was like one who faced the sinister portal of Death. And yet she was just going into the home the man who loved her had made for her, because he could not bring her into his.

He opened the door with his latchkey, and stood aside to let her pass in!

"Welcome!" he said.

She clutched his arm. She would not enter.

A HAPPY ENDING

"Oh, Tony, be good to me!" She shivered like a frightened dog. "Be good to me. Won't you? Be good to me."

"My God! Marcelle! How could I be else to you? My dear! My own dear! How could I be else?"

A man or woman of the world would have seen that this was acting, and excellent acting, but the blonde girl took it for genuine profound emotion and was comforted by it. She gave him just one glance and went in.

It was an apartment such as a young bride might dream of—neat spacings of white enamelled wood, a multitude of cushions, sunshine through the snowy curtains, and a caroling bird in a cage. A black-uniformed maid flitted down the corridor.

"I'm afraid, Tony. I'm afraid."

"You're afraid of letting your heart lead you. Don't be afraid of that, my dear, my own dear! My God! If only——"

She laid her hand quickly on his sleeve. She forgot herself in his misery.

"I know, my heart—that wretched woman. Oh, poor boy! If she would only set you free!"

"Some day she may di——"

A HAPPY ENDING

"Don't, Tony—not even of her."

He rose to go. Suddenly his words became practical.

"And you know the reason I couldn't have you wait. You must have your chance. Theatrical men in this town are impressed only by 'front,' as they call it. You have your apartment. You have your car. You have the best clothes shops can give you. And that counts immensely, Marcelle. If Bernhardt or Duse were to walk into a Broadway office shabby, they would say, 'She can't be a great actress. If she were she'd be getting the money. And if a woman gets money she spends it on herself.' That's the sort of brains on Broadway."

"I know, Tony, I know."

"And another thing you have—another asset, my own. You have the light in your face of a woman who is loved—the glamour of sunrise."

"Tony, dear!"

"I'm going now, Marcelle. I'll be back—this evening."

She rose and clutched his arm. Her face was very white.

"Be good to me, Tony, for our dear Lord's sake, be good to me! You don't know—you'll never know what this means to me. I'm just—a country girl,

A HAPPY ENDING

and they brought me up so strictly. You see—oh, just be good to me, Tony! Be very good to me. . . ."

There were lines about her eyes—fatigue. There was a droop to her mouth—disappointment. It had been a long, long day. She had sat for hours in theatrical managers' offices, only for a boy to come out, and say, "Mr. Lewissohn is gone for the day;" or to be received for a minute and told: "Oh, Miss Foster! Nothing yet. Call again, won't you—this day week, shall we say?" Or she had listened to fat, bald men who eyed her slim comeliness with favour, called her "sister," and told her she had made a hit with them, and ended up with "Gi' me a li'l kiss. C'me on. Be nice to me an' I'll be nice to you. Hey? How about it?"

The only thing that had kept up her courage and patience was the appointment to have dinner with Mr. Van Stetter—Tony, she blushed, as she had agreed to call him, when they decided that two such good friends would not stand on too much ceremony with each other.

"No luck?" he asked her when she entered the lounge of the hotel where they were to dine.

"Not yet," she smiled bravely.

"You saw Watson?" He had given her a note to the manager who had the reputation of making

A HAPPY ENDING

stars by tuition instead of by hackney play-writers and lavish advertisement.

"He told me to call later in the season. He was very nice to me," she answered hopefully.

And so Watson had his orders to be. But he and a half-dozen others were instructed she was to get no part. The Van Stetter millions are in a huge granite bank downtown, guarded with steel and electricity. But their vibrations reach far afield. A counsel for the Powhatan Bank may be also counsel for a theatrical syndicate. A vice-president of the Van Stetter combination may not be above taking a few paltry thousands for acting as angel to a sure-fire production. However it is done, the grip of Van Stetter on the theatrical profession is just as firm as on the automobile industry. He is a power on Broadway.

"What drew us together," he told Marcelle over the sole and sherry, "is we both want something big. You want to be the greatest actress in America. I wanted something just as big. I missed my want. I wish to help you get to yours. A little desire for a vicarious triumph—in you."

"But you, Mr. Van Stetter—Tony," she corrected herself prettily. "How can you want anything?"

"Oh, yes, I know," he laughed. "I am one of the richest men in the world—one of the most powerful;

A HAPPY ENDING

young; fêted everywhere; with a wife who is acknowledged to be the most beautiful woman in the East"—there was an edge of steel in his voice—"and yet—I have missed the greatest thing."

"Tell me!"—she leaned towards him with her gentle kindliness. "Tell me, your friend, Tony."

"You would think me a sentimental fool, or worse, a man starting a cheap flirtation. And I don't want you to think wrong of me."

"Tell me!" she insisted gently.

"I have never been loved—entirely—by a woman I loved. That is the greatest thing in life, Marcelle, to love your husband utterly, and be loved by him. Ah, well! Let's talk of your career."

He told her of the tremendous study she must go through to achieve her ambition. He told her of stage technique. He spoke of the Duse, whom he had seen in Italy; of Modjeska, whom he had seen in London; of Bernhardt, whom he knew.

"There is another little thing, Marcelle, someone will have to tell you. And I would rather do it, because I am your friend, and I don't want another to break it to you coarsely. To depict life for men and women of the world, you must know it. You must draw on the dynamos of life. You must know

A HAPPY ENDING

not only the glamour and sheen of love, but you must know the depths and power of it. You must have felt that yourself, utterly. Do you understand?"

She was blushing faintly. "I think I do," she faltered. "I—I think so."

"The great actress does not get this knowledge in domesticity. Domesticity she cannot afford. She is the privileged one. She must venture outside pale and boundary so that others may be taught and warned and led. For her the rule—what the sheltered people call morals—must be suspended."

"So"—Marcelle's voice was very low and troubled—"so I have read, or heard somewhere." Her head was lowered, and a slow carmine passed over her forehead.

"I only trust that when you go this path you must walk, that he who goes with you will be gentle and tactful and kind, and that you and he only go it because he loves you and you him."

"Thank you, Tony. Thank you!"

Before they left the restaurant she laid her hand on his arm.

"About that want of yours, Tony, that never came true. I think I understand. And I'm sorry about it, Tony. From my heart I'm sorry."

A HAPPY ENDING

She sat in a sort of frozen terror, while the train stood still at the station. Would it never go out? she asked herself. Then the bell of the locomotive began to toll, and with a jerk they were under way. She was free at last. None could stop her now.

She turned to her suitcase, and looked at it ruefully. The lock had unsnapped again, and its contents gaped through the open edges. She settled herself to the task of closing it.

She braced her knee against it, and pulled on the straps. But while it would close at the corners, the centre would not meet sufficiently. Her long hands had not the power in wrist and fingers to compress the centrifugal mass and snap the lock fast.

"Oh, darn!" She gave it up.

"Please let me." A bulky, smiling man from a neighbouring chair leaned past her and closed the case with a grip like a vice.

"Thank you," Marcelle said. "I didn't have time to pack properly."

"Few eloping girls do."

His smile was a friendly, gentle thing. One could not take offence.

"How do you know?"

A HAPPY ENDING

"Seen 'em before. Woods are full of 'em. Stage or matrimony?"

She liked him. She liked him at once. He took the whole thing so easily, so much in the spirit of adventurous fun.

"Stage," she smiled back merrily.

He looked at her critically. Few men could have done it without appearing either rude or mawkish. He was polite and entirely impersonal.

"The stage's the gainer," he decided succinctly.

"How do you know?"

"I know hundreds of stage folk. I know a dozen theatrical managers. The stage has swallowed up a good many dollars of my hard-earned money."

"You're not in the profession yourself."

"No," he said, as though regretfully. He took a card from his pig-skin fold. "Antony Van Stetter, 3rd," she read. She gave a gasp of awe.

"You're not——" she paused.

"I am that unfortunate man." His smile and friendliness wiped out the majesty that should surround him. He was—just folks.

"Your hard-earned money!" Marcelle scoffed with a humorous glance at him.

She was surprised to find he was sitting beside

A HAPPY ENDING

her in the next chair. It had all been done so easily, she hadn't noticed.

"Now tell me all about it," he instructed. "I love adventurers and I love the theatre. Tell me all about your plans. I'd be sincerely interested. Maybe I can help. . . ."

The first May moon was in the sky, pale as honey, thin as a dagger. The stars were out, infinite, liquid blueness. Along the country road were the faint delicate perfumes of Springtime. Marcelle had no time to admire them. She was half walking, half running, bent sideways under the weight of the heavy suitcase, fearful she might not catch her train, fearful that she would have to wait long on the platform, the cynosure of neighbours' eyes, and fearful, too, that her presence would be missed, and that someone would come out of the farm-house to see whither she had gone. There was very little probability of any of these things happening. But nevertheless she was afraid of interference at the eleventh hour.

Her plans had been made very well. When she got to New York, at Grand Central, she would invoke the Travellers' Aid Society, and they would assist her in getting a cheap and clean place to live. She would

A HAPPY ENDING

give them a fictitious name and address. And tomorrow she would go the rounds of the theatrical managers, whose names she had culled from a stage periodical. There would be no difficulty, getting a part. At a neighbouring town she had seen play after play tried out before its New York appearance, and she knew—how could she but know, unless she were a fool?—that she could do better than nine out of ten women on the stage. She had better looks. She had better carriage. She was a lady. And she knew her Shakespeare by heart.

The family would be hurt and shocked when they read the note saying she had gone to become an actress—but how proud they would be a year or so from now, when Broadway blazoned her name, and the papers were full of interviews about her art!

Good Lord! There was the train!

She put on a sprint of speed to make it, the suitcase banging her knees. Only a hundred and fifty yards to go to the station. She'd make it yet. There were others in as great a hurry. An eight-cylinder car roared behind, with imperative crash of horn. She moved to get out of its way. She tripped over her suitcase and came down dazedly on hands and knees. Something struck her then, and there was a vast explosion, and she was riven from the roots of earth.

A HAPPY ENDING

Then suddenly she discovered herself erect, light as a zephyr, with the moon and stars on either hand—one of the great and ghostly Audience, which watches, in its leisure moments, the sordid tragedy, the empty comedy, the miserable mumming on the stage called life. . . .

The station agent, the local truckman, and a couple of passengers raced towards the body. Beside it were the terrified chauffeur and the flustered occupant of the car. The station agent knelt down, stood up.

"It's Zeke Foster's girl," he discovered. "Her that was to college."

"Dead?"

"Yes, sir. She's dead."

The truckman drew the agent aside.

"Know who's in the car?"

"Don't know."

"That city millionaire that has the woman up to the Myers' bungalow. That's who it is!"

"Judas Priest!" the agent swore. "Ain't it the heck to think of a girl like Zeke Foster's girl being killed by a squirt like that, on his way home from that light woman of hisn! The ways of Providence," he philosophized, "they sure beat me!"

IV

A CERTAIN REGRETTABLE OCCASION

I

NEW YORK and Ireland and all the world had forgotten old Patrick Monahan, but he was still alive. In the third story of the big house on Madison Avenue he had his rooms. He got out of bed feebly, and ate meals, and went back again. Occasionally he was driven here and there in a big limousine, but the exertion tried him. He didn't care to go out much. He preferred to sit still and dream about Ireland.

His son and daughters, and their sons and daughters, loomed large in the public prints. James Monahan was a director of a big bank and head of the construction company his father had founded, but the elder men in New York knew him to be less than a shadow of the old father.

"If Pat hadn't made the money, James wouldn't have it now. That big, empty head would be floor

A CERTAIN REGRETTABLE OCCASION

walker in a departmental store. It's a pity old Pat died!"

"But he isn't dead. Old Pat isn't dead."

"You don't tell me! You don't mean old Pat is still alive? I thought he'd been dead this twenty years."

He was all but dead. A compact figure of a man, strangely unsupple, beneath his white beard his face showed mottled here and there. He was eighty-five and all he was doing was dreaming and waiting for death.

But his dreams were not of his marriage, or of the days when he builded a great part of New York and was a power in the land. They were of earlier days in Ireland, and of the one tremendous deed he had done there, that none except his son and daughters knew about.

More clearly now than the day after the event he could remember waiting in the dusk in the lane near Lucan, hidden in the hedgerow, cuddling his gun between his knees. Then there was the snapping trot of the barouche, and the English Viceroy of Ireland had appeared leaning back on the cushions, and a friend on the seat before him. Monahan had waited calmly until the carriage was opposite him, and the aim he took was very

A CERTAIN REGRETTABLE OCCASION

deliberate. He fired both barrels as calmly as though shooting snipe, and the Viceroy of Ireland was a dead man.

II

"Nobody ever knew who did that deed," he used to tell James, his son. "There were three of us in it, and for a month they scoured the country looking for the villains, and the three of us all the time walking Dublin streets. Then it became dangerous, and each of us went our way. Number Two got killed on a railroad track, and Number Three entered a Trappist monastery, but I got down to Waterford and from Waterford to France, and from France across to America. A new Viceroy came and if they had had any luck they'd have killed him too. But they didn't hang together. There was a traitor among them. There's always a traitor to spoil a man's plans. He mayn't betray you for money, but he'll do it for some reason or other. A traitor is a terrible thing."

James would listen to him politely, a trifle bored. If he could have afforded it he would not have paid any attention or courtesy to the old man, but his father was the only one who had the money, and so

A CERTAIN REGRETTABLE OCCASION

he had to be listened to. The fact that Patrick Monahan was recounting a murder he had committed gleefully didn't please the son. That was his father's affair. It was so far away, so long ago.

"Our plan of campaign was to kill them off as soon as they were appointed, until they got sick of sending Viceroys and terrified at what would happen. By then they would know they couldn't rule Ireland, and they might have let her go. Aye, sure, they would have let her go. What's the sense or profit in keeping a wolf in your backyard? Better open wide the gates and let him go."

The old man would take a pull at his pipe, and survey the son shrewdly.

"I had thought when you were born that maybe I had a son who could go back with my money and help carry on the good work. But there's not enough steel in you, Jamie, not enough steel."

James Monahan was not of the type to be insulted, nevertheless. It was all one to him whether the old man considered him of steely piles or not. He had his own ambitions, though he never spoke of them to his father. He did not understand what actuated the elder Monahan. Even if he had he wouldn't have cared.

A CERTAIN REGRETTABLE OCCASION

Raised on a Connaught bog, the earliest thing Patrick Monahan had heard was the story of how the Irish tribes had been driven to "hell or Connaught" at the point of Cromwell's sword. A poor place Connaught was, and is to this day. Except for certain stretches here and there, it is a region of bogs and bleak mountains, of barren soil and raging sea—cold grey stones and a mist that seems the end of the world. There is magnificent scenery there, and the colours of sunrise and sunset are blended into startling blues and yellows, superb gold and palpable purple. But it is no place for men to live and breed and eat in; with no sustenance but the granite soil.

In the byways of Connaught there is a certain question always asked of a stranger.

"Did you ever in all your travels see a poorer place nor this place?" And the traveller is constrained to answer that he never did.

A strange people, they of Connaught, with a far away expression in their eyes. Foreigners visiting them, and watching the brooding look, talk about the Celtic twilight and the mysticism of the Irish peasant. They think they are dreaming of vague gods and goddesses by some pearly shore, and they write poems and books about them.

A CERTAIN REGRETTABLE OCCASION

But they are not dreaming of mythologies, they are thinking of very palpable things. They are remembering the fields from which they were driven centuries before by torch and sword and arquebuss. They remember the fertile orchard lands of Ulster, and Leinster, swarming with heavy kine, Munster broad-bosomed and lush with green grass. Once that land was theirs, as the land flowing with milk and honey was the portion of exiled Israel. Israel had thrived in exile but Connaught has not. Israel rules the mart but Connaught has only a few inches of soil to grow potatoes and its chance of the fleeting herring shoal.

And there was the famine, too, the year when the crops died and men and women died in the ditches of the roadside because of it. Connaught cannot forget that.

And there is only one cause and one race that Connaught blames, rightly or wrongly, for its subjection and its poverty, and that is England. And as it is nearly impossible to concentrate sufficient hatred on a whole race, it picks one tangible person, the King of England, for the searing venom. But the King of England is a far way off, in his Tower of London, with his Dukes and his Beefeaters, his guards and ordnance. And there is no chance of reaching him.

A CERTAIN REGRETTABLE OCCASION

But his shadow and deputy is in Ireland, his Lord Lieutenant, his Viceroy, the Vice-King. In Dublin town he wears the robes of royalty, and in Dublin castle he holds court, a levée of peers and peeresses that is to London as the moon is to the sun. But it is the royalty of England rules, and the Lord Lieutenant is King of Ireland, subject to his sovereign lord.

When Patrick Monahan was a young man, there had just been the Famine, and Connaught and all Ireland seethed with the desire to drive the English into the sea. There were various plans of campaign, some of them legislative, some of them revolutionary. In those old days there were no Local Government Boards or Fishery Commissions or agricultural societies to help the Connaught people. There was nothing but poverty and oppression and a vast resentment, so there were many with Patrick Monahan and his associates who saw no murder but plain execution in what the young rebel did, when he crouched with his blunderbuss in a hedgerow, and put two neat holes through the vitals of the King's deputy.

The old man opened a newspaper to the page where was a picture of the present viceroy and his wife. "Irish Lord Lieutenant to visit America," went the newspaper heading. "Will conciliate Irish Americans

A CERTAIN REGRETTABLE OCCASION

while here." A tall, thin man, a Welsh peer, he had the vacuous look and drooping moustaches of the English county officer.

"If there were men in Ireland, himself would be a dead man," old Patrick Monahan murmured. "I'd do him in as quick as I'd look at him. I did in one of them. I'd do in the whole tribe."

III

There was one passion in James Monahan's life, and that was to be important.

If you were to watch that man closely, you couldn't fail to see the ambition exuding from him like resin from a tree. A tall, thin man, with an extremely wise manner and a sententious utterance, with pale blue eyes that challenged you as a small dog may challenge a St. Bernard. You could not but feel that here was a person who wanted you to have a certain opinion of him, who wanted to sell you himself, as the business men say, as a person of high rating in the community and that community the world.

"Oh, James is all right," his business associates would say with a smile, and that smile meant that

A CERTAIN REGRETTABLE OCCASION

James was just to be laughed at, not liked, not hated, not even despised, just to be laughed at.

What his associates thought James Monahan didn't care. It was what the wide world thought. He would have liked to have walked down Broadway or Fifth Avenue and around Wall Street, and have people point him out, as they would point out Mr. Rockfeller or Signor Caruso.

"That's James Monahan," his ambition could hear them whisper.

The men who knew his father and who knew him said he had no brains, no anything, "Just a mess," as they phrased it. But he had a certain instinctive cunning. He could not be a great figure in business, he knew that. His function was to sit on boards while his father's lieutenants guarded the Monahan holdings. He could not be a power in politics. He had no personality, no ideas.

At Y.M.C.A. clubhouses and at young men's gatherings he was often called on to give addresses on moral subjects which his secretary would write for him, and which he would intone in a dry and unconvincing manner. But this did not get him very far.

The social world was the only one he could hope to cut any swathe in, and when he was young he had

A CERTAIN REGRETTABLE OCCASION

purposed marrying a woman who would get him on. But all his father's money could not tempt a poverty-stricken social family to admit that lukewarm alkali personality into their midst, so he had to be content with marrying the daughter of old Hires, the shingle man, a fat, sheep-like woman with a certain fair prettiness, whose shining virtue was docility, and who considered any decision he arrived at a revelation from Mount Sinai.

When he brought his bride-to-be to his father the old man could hardly refrain from laughing.

"There was only one woman in the world for you, James, and that's Clara. Now that you've got one another, you ought to be happy." He looked at them for an instant. "By cripes! You make a great team."

But James didn't mind. He knew his father was laughing at him. Let him laugh if that did him any good.

He was a sincerely pious man, and his religion to some extent rewarded him for his charity and piety. There was never a moment that his cheque-book —his father's money—was not at the disposal of a worthy ecclesiastical project. The Irish Exiles' Bank—his father's—took care of church investments, and James was rewarded with a knighthood of

A CERTAIN REGRETTABLE OCCASION

Saint Gregory, and at certain functions, visits of nuncios, the consecration of bishops and the like, he was present in his splendid uniform, with his sword and star. His picture was often in denominational papers.

But that was not sufficient. He wanted something wider, something that would give him an entry into the big affairs of the day. He never spoke of it to his father, but the old man knew.

Old Patrick was never weary of looking at the picture of the visiting viceroy. He dissected the features bitterly, and cursed the man with all the savagery of his Connaught heritage.

"By jabers! if I was a young man, he'd no sooner set foot in New York than he'd be carried home heels first." He turned to his son. "Why don't you go out and blow that man's head off, the way I did and me hardly more than half your age. That would get you talked about," he laughed. "By cripes! That would get your picture in the paper."

His son said nothing, but regarded the old man with his vacant, inscrutable smile.

A CERTAIN REGRETTABLE OCCASION

IV

The stocky, keen-eyed doctor looked at the old man in the bed. He turned to James.

"I'll tell you the exact truth, Mr. Monahan," he said, "your father may last ten years, or he may last a month, or he may last a day. If you are certain to keep all excitement away from him, he will be all right. One burst of excitement and he's a dead man."

"But he gets no excitement, no worry," James said.

"Well, you must see to it that he doesn't."

Old Patrick, half asleep, half delirious, tossed on the bed.

"By cripes! I done in one of them, and I'd do in this one. Begor! there was men in Ireland in my day!"

"Would you let him see the papers?"

"If there's anything in them to excite him, I would not.

"I see." James smiled his vacuous, inscrutable smile.

The son went into the library after the physician had left and rang up a newspaper number.

A CERTAIN REGRETTABLE OCCASION

"Is Mr. Grogan there?"

Grogan was an excellent reporter, who also did a great deal of publicity work on the side, as the phrase is. Occasionally he was hired to help out a play that seemed doomed to failure, occasionally to raise interest in a foreign lecturer in America, and not infrequently to scatter propaganda of various kinds in the public Press.

"Grogan, I am told you have charge of Lord Llewdyth's lecture tour over here. How is it going?"

"Why, not very well, Mr. Monahan. The ordinary public are interested in him, but the Irish Americans fight shy."

"I was thinking, Grogan, of inviting Lord and Lady Llewdyth to dinner at my house. Do you think that could be managed?"

"Why, I think so, Mr. Monahan, but——" the reporter's voice was instinct with surprise.

"But what, Grogan?"

"Your father, Mr. Monahan?" Grogan knew vaguely that the elder Monahan had been implicated in a great political crime in Ireland though none knew exactly what it was. The old man was prominent as a bitter enemy of alien rule in Ireland. "Your father, what does he say?"

A CERTAIN REGRETTABLE OCCASION

"My father," James Monahan purred, "will be delighted. Of course you will understand he will not be there. He is an old man, a sick man. But things are changed, Grogan. The old days of the Irreconcilables and the Invincibles are gone. Ireland is the most prosperous country in the world, and it only needs a little diplomacy, a little tact, to make a bridge. Myself, as probably the most prominent Irish American in New York, am willing to help this cause. I think it is my public duty."

"I think I can arrange it, Mr. Monahan."

"Do. There's a good fellow, Grogan. And please let me know as soon as possible."

He hung up the receiver, and rubbed his hands, smiling his vacant, inscrutable smile. A viceroy, the next thing to a king, entertained at his house. Now the world should sit up and take notice of James Monahan.

v

Grogan burst into the Viceroy's hotel suite full of importance.

"Well, your Excellency. I've arranged something big."

A CERTAIN REGRETTABLE OCCASION

"You don't mean it? You don't say so." The Lord Lieutenant smiled his set viceregal smile.

"Yes, sir. I've got a dinner invitation for you and Lady Llewdyth from James Monahan."

"You don't mean it? James Monahan?"

"You know who James Monahan is, of course."

"The name is, of course, familiar, but——"

"He is the son of Patrick Monahan, the rebel."

"You don't say so. Patrick Monahan, the rebel."

"Patrick Monahan, your Excellency will remember, was implicated in that unfortunate affair in Dublin when one of your predecessors was unfortunately killed."

"You don't mean it. You don't say so. And you think I ought to accept?"

"Undoubtedly. The effect on the whole Irish-American public will be of incalculable value."

"You don't mean it. You don't say so."

"It will be in the nature of a state reconciliation."

"You don't tell me. Patrick Monahan and the Lucan murder. How very interesting indeed. I must accept then. What do you think? I must accept for myself and the Vicereine."

A CERTAIN REGRETTABLE OCCASION

VI

The old man turned to the pretty black-haired nurse.

"Listen now, my dear. If you want to go to your friend's wedding this evening, just slip off and say nothing to anybody. I'll be fine."

"I'm afraid, Mr. Monahan."

"I'm grand. You can see yourself. And I'll be fine."

"I'm afraid. But if I thought——"

"Go on now, my dear."

"Thank you, Mr. Monahan." She moved about the room fixing up medicine bottles, tidying up, performing the details of her profession. The old man spoke again.

"Did you find out why they've got the red awning over the sidewalk?"

"I didn't hear, sir."

James came in rubbing his hands.

"Who's been married in this house, James Monahan?" his father demanded.

"Nobody."

"Then why the red awning?"

A CERTAIN REGRETTABLE OCCASION

"The red awning! Oh, yes! The red awning. Oh, just some people to dinner to-night."

"By cripes! They must be royalty for you to have that out."

"Oh, no!" James laughed easily. "Not exactly."

"One of your princes of the church, maybe."

"Yes, yes. Just a dignitary of kinds. Now, father, you mustn't excite yourself. Don't ask any questions."

"I ought to know what's going on in my own house," old Patrick grumbled.

"Mr. Monahan, you've got to take your nap now," the nurse instructed. James left the room.

The old man drowsed more than ordinarily. When he awoke he was alone and night had set in. The blinds were drawn and a subdued light shone on a dressing table. Miss Kane, the nurse, had gone.

"I wonder what's going on downstairs," old Patrick murmured. He grumbled viciously. Damn those doctors! They could insist a man was sick when he wasn't at all. He wondered what was going on downstairs.

"I wonder who James has got in his net now," he laughed. And the thought came to him he would never know, and that worried him. His son provided the old man with a great deal of amusement,

A CERTAIN REGRETTABLE OCCASION

and the thought that he would not be able to bait James to-morrow disappointed the ancient rebel. He loved to mimic James, "Yes, your Grace!" or "Yes, your Honour," or "Mr. Alderman," or "If I may speak as a man not of unimportance in certain circles."

By cripes! He'd just have to find out what it was about.

He got up and groped around until he found his dressing gown and slippers. He was surprised to feel how well he was, but as he made his way down the second flight of stairs the sweat broke out on his brow and the top of his mouth was dry as baked clay. For several instants he thought he would have to call for help but that he remembered would get Miss Kane into trouble. So he sat on the stairs until he was rested and made his way to the hall. The maid in uniform started as she saw him.

"Oh, Mister Patrick."

"Arrah, whisht your mouth!" he told her fiercely, and made his way toward the dining-room. His knees wavered.

"By cripes! It's me is the old man!"

The dining-room was slightly open, and as he looked through it, for all his years he stiffened like a setter. He recognised from the pictures in the paper

A CERTAIN REGRETTABLE OCCASION

the man and woman who sat by James' side, the thin viceroy with the vacuous look and the drooping moustaches and the plump, dark-haired peeress with the iron eyes.

"By cripes!" old Patrick gasped. "It's me is the betrayed man!"

Some strange, sinister energy was distilled then in the antique frame and he made his way back up the stairs with as seeming ease as he had done it twenty years before. He gained his own bedroom.

"The dirty dog! he snarled. "And him a son of Patrick Monahan!"

He rummaged in a cupboard until he found what he wanted, a double barrelled gun, of the old muzzle-loading type with percussion caps to explode the charge. The gun was the one he had used in Lucan generations before, and it had been his hobby to keep it as well-oiled, its charges as exact and fresh, its percussion caps as new as in the old days. "*Bas gan Sogarth*" he called it familiarly—"Death without the priest," and when the son rallied him on the care he gave to the grisly memento, he would laugh and say there might be need for it again.

"It's me is the careful man," he said grimly as he started for the door.

A CERTAIN REGRETTABLE OCCASION

There would be one barrel for the viceroy and one for James he promised himself. Dinner! He'd give them their bellyfull of death.

As he came to the top of the flight of stairs to the hall, he paused. His heart was acting strangely. One moment it seemed to inflate like a balloon and the next to contract to the size of a nut. And strange waves swept over him, trying to pluck the life out of his body. His body was a rack and the life attached to it by a thin filament, and the waves tried to snatch the life away angrily.

"They'll be dead men down there in a minute, and then the waves can have me."

But another wave came crashing towards him, the seventh wave.

"By cripes!" And he fell the length of the stairs.

VII

The maid from the hall rushed in to the dining-room with white, staring face. She threw her apron suddenly over her face.

"*A wirr is throo!*" she shrieked. "*A wirr is throo!* O Virgin Mary! What a pity."

James rose. "I trust your Excellencies will

A CERTAIN REGRETTABLE OCCASION

pardon me," he smiled. He followed the girl into the hall.

He saw the body of the old man in the dressing gown lying over the antique gun. He bent forward and felt his heart. Patrick Monahan was dead.

He rose without a tremor. " Get him upstairs," he directed the maid. "Get the rest to help you and get him upstairs. And not a word!" he threatened. He returned to the table.

"I trust nothing is wrong, Mr. Monahan. I trust so indeed," the Viceroy hoped kindly.

"Nothing of importance, your Excellency. An old—sort of dependant of the family had a—sort of accident."

"You don't mean it. You don't say so."

"Well, about the mass meeting of Irish Americans, your Excellency. I should be very glad to take the chair and introduce you. As a person of not unimportance in certain circles; as the son of Patrick Monahan, the rebel, who, as your Excellency knows, was mixed up," he smiled coyly, "on a certain regrettable occasion."

V

ANTI-CLIMAX

THE ladies' quartet—the three golden-haired girls and the brunette, who had plucked out most giftedly the quaint Indian tunes in minor—had left the stage. In the new mammoth moving-picture house the serried audience moved and settled with a sound as of a great wind soughing. Before the ladies' quartet had come on, there had been shown a film of an internationally popular harlequin, a quaint, somewhat vulgar fellow, but an artist, with a billy-cock hat and a trick stick and a grotesque moustache. That had been looked forward to; been heartily enjoyed. But that was overshadowed by what was going to occur now—the *première* of a film picture featuring Julia Montagu. As a minor thrill there was to be with her Roy Kenton, the handsomest young lead in the movies.

Aloft, in the handsome, gold-leaved boxes, sat a British Consul-General; the Chancellor in New York of the Ottoman Empire; a Broadway personage famous for his diamonds; a Judge of the Supreme

ANTI-CLIMAX

Court and the Mayor of New York. Without, the theatre crowds still patiently and optimistically filed to the box-office; looked crestfallen; shrugged their shoulders; moved away. Below in the pit the dapper conductor rapped his stand and the orchestra of forty-eight pieces broke softly into a faint melody with a clangorous Oriental barbarism hidden somewhere back of it. The house darkened. The cinematograph shot forward a beam of white like a searchlight.

"Julia Montagu in *Black Magic*," and then followed a list of directors, photographers, scenario writers, and author. "Roy Kenton as Lieutenant-Commander Jennings, U.S.N.; Neil Campbell as Hadji Achmet Hassan."

The machine above commenced to purr like some well-oiled engine. The soughing susurrus of the house's interest dropped suddenly. In the dark young couples began to grope for each other's hands, and the elder people sat back with sighs of contentment. The picture took form and life. . . .

How long is it, I wonder, since Julia Montagu played that last great scene of hers, and quitted us all in one dramatic exit? It cannot be more than four or five years ago—more probably four. The years pass by now fast as a mill-race, whirling

ANTI-CLIMAX

onward like a comet, burying great names and glorious ideals, and shivering massive facts.

Great fighters are forgotten, great heroes, great preachers. Anon comes Time, and obliterates their names even on their carven tombs. But one trade remains alone, most evanescent of all, the names of whose lights are never forgotten. There will never be forgotten the names of Kendal and Siddons, and of Bernhardt and Modjeska and the Duse. Those will be always remembered—those, and the name of Julia Montagu!

You can still remember Julia Montagu as she appeared many hundred times on Broadway—a slim, lissome figure of a girl, even at thirty-three. Her head was small, and her neck white and graceful as a swan's. You will remember the torrent of black hair she had, so much of it as to appear enormous; the very dusky dark eyes, large, sunk in a smudge of black shadow; the small, decided features; the highish cheekbones; the generous, whimsical mouth. She was less than beautiful and more than pretty—much more.

"Bonny!" she was once described by a playgoer of the ancient school, an old gentleman with exquisite manners. That was the only word to describe her! Bonny! "The bonniest thing that ever trod the boards."

ANTI-CLIMAX

The public never knew—until that last night—who she was and where she came from. Echstein, who found her in a small part in a comedy in London, never said much about her. It may have been diffidence on his part, or it may have been business—you never could tell with Echstein.

"She's an actress," he would tell you. "She's a great actress. She's the best actress in the English-speaking world"—that was going a bit far. "Her private affairs are none of your blasted business."

And so many legends grew up about Julia Montagu—from the Austrian Archduchess legend of 1908 to the theory that she was the offspring of a scrubwoman in Vandewater Street. To all questions she would smile her whimsical smile and reply in her accent that was neither English, Irish, Scotch, nor God-fearing American:

"Indeed, what does it matter who I am?" she would plead. "All I want to do is good work for the public. Can't you let me be about that?"

But other things the public learned about her, and for them it took her to its bosom. It learned that always her purse was open to any pitiful appeal, and not ostentatiously but secretly. It learned that at the sight of a cripple on the street her great dark eyes would fill with tears. One of the half-dozen

ANTI-CLIMAX

times her name was on a front page was when she caught a coloured driver lashing a galled horse on a steep street between Riverside Drive and Broadway.

"Come down!" She stepped out of her car and approached the man. "Come down before I tear you down!"

The man clambered down in a sort of stupefaction. She snatched the heavy whip from his hand, her eyes blazing. She motioned to her chauffeur.

"Get me a policeman, quick, Tom," she told him.

"But I can't leave you alone, Miss," he objected,

"The only danger is to him!" she snapped.

And bravely she had him arrested for cruelty to the poor galled and spavined old crock; and bravely, too, she appeared against him next day. Casimir, the most lenient magistrate in New York, was for sending him to the electric chair when she appeared. But he sent the man to the Island. And while he was there Julia Montagu paid his wages to his family.

New York, cynical, worldly-wise, would have laughed and hinted at a press-agent had another actress done these things. When it leaked out that she read a chapter of the Bible at night and attended

ANTI-CLIMAX

a quiet little church on the upper West Side, instead of grinning it shook its head solemnly, as though it recognized that though this was a queer thing, it was all right if one felt that way. When it came to the ears of part of New York that she was in the habit of dropping into a hospital for crippled children, without chauffeur or chow dog or other appanage, that part of New York blubbered outright.

"I'll tell you what she is," a hardened Broadwayite, exceedingly suspicious and notoriously sinful, gave his opinion. "I'll tell you: She's a real old-fashioned girl, actress or no actress. That's what she is! I bet you that girl had a good father and mother. God love her, say I!"

Now, there are many excellent women with good hearts and kind dispositions—some of them better-looking than Julia Montagu, but New York did not notably enthuse over them. It enthused over Julia Montagu because she was a great actress and a bonny girl. And great actress she was! She made notable successes in the plays that Richard Bennett wrote for her — those technically perfect things revolving about one sweet, wronged woman. She played *Nell Gwynne* and *Heart of Corn*, and the Dutch *vrouw* in *The Burgher*, until she was sick,

ANTI-CLIMAX

sore and tired of them. And still Broadway clamoured for more.

Broadway went uncomplainingly to see her in *Romeo and Juliet*; to see her in *As You Like It*; to see her as Ophelia—her one failure. It voted Shakespeare all right for schools, but rather *vieux jeu* for the stage.

"But she's got to do it," Broadway surmised. "They all got to do it. Just to show they're class!"

It suffered patiently while she went on in the plays of the surly Norwegian dramatist, "the Ibsen gink" as New York called him. And then they saw acting. In *A Doll's House*; in *Hedda Gabler*; in *The Master Builder*; in *Ghosts*; they saw her quick, vibrant, tremulous, alive with passion and feeling from the smallest hair in her head to her finger-tips, to the minutest quaver in her voice. Understanding, they were thrilled. Something shuddered within them, as it might shudder at the actuality of tragedy. There is a picture somewhere —an advertising device—of a giant holding a handful of lightning. That handful of lightning—that was Julia Montagu.

"Believe me, boy!" it was said, "if that baby ever again gets a good play—you know what I

ANTI-CLIMAX

mean, a good play—she'll clean up like Hetty Green. It'll be all over but the shouting!"

I hardly think there was a man or boy in New York who was not in love with her in those days—not the blind passion that some actresses inspire, or the stunning infatuation of others, but a sweet and wholesome love. There were a thousand who proposed to her. Toward all she was very gentle; over some she cried.

"You're paying me the greatest compliment ever a man could pay," she would tell them, "but——"

"You can't marry me?" they would say.

"Maybe I'll never marry," she broke it easily.

But now, it was believed, her time for capitulation had come. From California, where she had been taking pictures, the rumour had arrived on Broadway that at last she had consented to marry Roy Kenton, her leading man in the movie business. It had been all but an assured thing before they had sailed for Morocco to film *Black Magic*. She had not been seen since the return, nor had he. But the papers had printed the rumour and been near to fact.

I don't know what the opinion of men was about Roy Kenton. I have an idea that few liked him. Tall, blonde, with magnificent, regular features and

ANTI-CLIMAX

grey eyes that photographed, he was undeniably the handsomest of the male movie stars. He was well-built, moved easily and gracefully, and had good manners—he never kept his hat on in a movie drawing-room. There were two things I didn't like about him. In front face you could not see his ears. I don't know what that denotes in phrenology, but it always gave me the feeling that his ears had been lopped off by the public hangman for some improper crime. Also his teeth curved inward. I may be wrong, but I never trust a man with that sort of teeth.

"What sort of a chap is this Roy Kenton?" was once asked of a cinematograph magnate. The answer was unsatisfactory.

"Uh-huh. You hear things—but I found him all right."

About his origin, as about the origin of Julia Montagu, there was a sort of mystery. He had never been on the legitimate stage, and was not the great public figure that Julia Montagu was, so the thing did not matter very much. It was said he was the natural son of a great Norse actress and a royal personage. It sounded romantic and was improbable, but he never denied it. It was also said that he was a younger son of a British noble family.

ANTI-CLIMAX

I don't know what the opinion of men was about Roy Kenton, but I know the opinion of women. To all of them, young and old, he represented the great ideal—the Fairy Prince who broke through the woods where the Sleeping Beauty lay. He was the nobleman with long moustaches of whom the housemaids dream; the Djinn of Wonders and terrible aspect whom a queen might desire, even while loving her harassed husband. He was the magic lover in the garden of souls. They liked the way he lounged and smoked his cigarette in his evening things; his manner of kissing a woman's hand; his noble, undaunted aspect as he faced the villain of the piece; his way of saving the heroine in the climax of the play; and they sighed gently and comfortably as he faded off against a sunset, against a clump of lilac bushes, against some Spanish tapestry, with the heroine's head on his shoulder.

And now to-night they were going to see their favourite screen lover make love to the little actress they had all taken to their hearts. To their ears had come the rumour—the definite knowledge they claimed it to be, in their optimistic way—that these twain were to be married and live happily ever after. There would be more than mumming in this, they knew. Above them the camera purred

ANTI-CLIMAX

and the light shot forward to the screen, and minute human shadowgraphs moved on the surface of mute, inscrutable Africa. Young girls thrilled with expectation, and into the eyes of elder women a faint moisture crept, as they thought of ancient springtime days, when, with the greening of boughs and the clear crescent moon, love pit-a-patted in their hearts, like the flutter of a bird's wing. . . .

It is a very difficult matter to describe a motion-picture story. What with their fade-aways, their cut-backs, their abrupt convolutions, they cover in a minute what a pen would take an hour to tell. *Black Magic* began with a Ball at Fortress Monroe, where white-clad Navy men danced with mysterious-eyed Southern girls. Prominent among the dancers was Lieutenant-Commander Jennings, U.S.N., who was Roy Kenton, and Charity Froude, daughter of Congressman Froude. They wandered out to a moonlit balcony. A blushing, gentle, delicate hint of love-making, and in gigantic majuscules on the screen you were told that Charity was going to accompany her father to Morocco in Africa on a trip for the sake of his health. Naturally, the Commander's boat is also going to Moroccan waters. It is probable that they will meet there. It faded off into a gentle, favourable beginning. People sat

ANTI-CLIMAX

back in their chairs comfortably. This was going to be good.

A short interview with her father that night in their Norfolk home, and you got the impression that Froude did not approve of Jennings. A bit of a waster, like his father, though an excellent officer. However. . . . You see Froude and Charity in Morocco, white-clad, moving against the shaded antique background. They are strange. They seem insolent in their Westernness. One feels the city brooding against them, resentful, sinister. Arabs pass by, haughty, sneering. One feels, somehow, as though the couple were innocuous insects dangerously near a spider's web.

A quick flash to the desert at sunset and one sees the dark Senyusseh lodges, where the outcast dervishes perform black magic. Through Africa has arisen the periodical chafing against the rule of the white men. Once again the Holy War is to be preached and the land purged of the infidel. But there is the memory of the Mahdi and of the other lost causes. In secrecy the leaders consult the occult freemasonry of Africa. They call to the aid of their clean-cut faith the abominations of necromancy. They are told that their cause will be successful if there be sacrificed on the altars of the evil gods,

ANTI-CLIMAX

which Islam does not recognize, a white virgin of the race they wish to conquer by fire and sword. The audience leaned forward. Their breaths came and went like the hissing of a small furnace.

Then stepped out on the screen Hadji Achmet Hassan, green-turbaned, white-robed, brown, lithe, unbelievably sinister, chosen leader of the great *jehad*. With his face that was berry-brown; with his great hook-nose and eyes that were scornful as an eagle's; with his firm-set mouth, firm-set jaw, and bull's neck; with his one great scar over the right cheekbone, and two fingers missing from his left hand, he gave the impression of an individual ruthless as Death. There is nothing repulsive about him. He is only too powerful. The audience shrank from him as from a drawn sword.

Onward the story rolled in its quick-thrilling climaxes. There was the capture of Charity Froude in the streets of Morocco—a quick scuffle and a squadron of Arabs flying into the desert against a huge, red, nearly-full moon. There was the father clamouring at the Consul's office. One saw Lieutenant-Commander Jennings on the bridge of the *Velocity* dreaming at sunset of the Ball at Fortress Monroe and looking forward to the meeting in Morocco.

ANTI-CLIMAX

From the black tents in the Sahara the word has gone forth into Egypt, into Tangier, into the great interiors, into Algiers of the French, that on the night of the waning moon the green banner of the Prophet is to be raised and the Holy War proclaimed. The dervishes of the Senyusseh lodge await a propitious moment for the supreme sacrifice. Hadji Achmet Hassan looks at the sacrifice.

He finds her fair, does Achmet Hassan Effendi, this daughter of the Frank. He has four wives already, as the Prophet permits, but he is willing to add the *giaour* girl to his *haremlik*. What does he care for sacrifices? With his sword he will be victorious. He pitches a silk handkerchief in the air, and cuts it in two with his scimitar. One sees the flash of the blade, and notes an arm of brown-bunched muscle, like the muscle of a hunting beast's leg. If she will, he will rescue her from the terrible priests. He advances toward her. She recoils. The audience breathes hard in vicarious horror.

I must skip the details of that picture. With pen and paper and a few words I cannot depict what took them two hours to show with their purring cameras and frenzied directors and great actors and hordes of beasts and men and the glamour of Africa to aid. That picture—you cannot have forgotten

ANTI-CLIMAX

it. You will remember the great scene in the Consul's office, where he pleads with Jennings to do nothing rash.

"Damn diplomacy!" you can see Jennings's lips frame. "I'm going to get that girl!"

You will remember how daringly he sneaked into the tent where she was kept, throttling the Arab sentinel from behind. You remember them fleeing toward Morocco and safely across the barren sandy wastes that undulate like waves. They rush onwards through the night. Dawn comes with tints of grey and rose and emerald. Overhead a marabout bird flaps by on heavy wings. The sun comes up suddenly like some gigantic crimson balloon. . . .

Back of them a single horseman appears, a black dot against the skyline. You can see his Arab stallion fly over the sand like a racing engine. You see his face. It is Achmet Hassan, who has outstripped all pursuers. In a final effort Jennings turns to face the preacher of the Holy War. The Arab springs to the ground. He drops his heavy rhinoceros-hide whip. There is hate in his eyes as he looks at the naval officer—stark, undeniable hate. He spits an insult at the man. He turns to catch the girl. Jennings catches up the *sjambok* and lashes the Arab across the face.

ANTI-CLIMAX

It was a cruel thing to do, and there was no hidden mystery of photography in it, for you saw the white weal start out across the man's face. The audience jumped in their seats in a sudden start of nerves. But they quickly forgot it. The man deserved no sympathy! He was a dog! the audience voted.

A quick grapple between Achmet Hassan and Jennings. You saw Jennings's knuckles smash home over the Arab's eye; cut the brow. One felt that the Hadji could easily have broken the white man's back, but he went down throttled. He lay very still. Above him circled one solitary bird.

Jennings had captured the Arab horse and had swung into the saddle. He leaned forward to lift up Charity. In an instant, you felt, she would be in his arms, her head against his shoulder, and there would be a tender love scene, which would fade away against the crimson dawn. . . .

Down the aisle came the sound of excited voices —a man's voice, pleading, panicky; a woman's, tense, excited. The audience turned wrathfully. A vast "Hush" came from the house.

The fat, benevolent little manager with the bald head and the close-cropped brown moustache was waving his hands.

ANTI-CLIMAX

"I ask you: do me the favour," he kept pleading. "I ask you."

"I will go up!" came the woman's voice passionately.

"I ask you——"

There was the patter of steps down the aisle and up the little stairs to the left of the stage a woman ran. She came out before the flickering camera. For an instant the picture covered her with weird streakings like those of a disguised ship. The operator stared a moment in astonishment. He shut off the picture. She stood out against the white glare.

"It's Julia Montagu!" somebody cried.

For a minute the house rocked with hand-clapping like rifle-fire. There was the dull mutter of comment and talk like the mutter of the sea on the shore. A man cheered up in the balcony and a man below answered. Suddenly the house rang with insane applause. She put up her hand pleadingly. Very gradually the thunder of approval ceased.

"Thank you!" she said. There was a queer little glitter in her eye. "This is the first time I have seen this picture, just like yourselves—and before it ends I just had to come up and say something——"

ANTI-CLIMAX

The manager broke in, standing at the first row of stalls.

"I ask you, Miss Montagu, do me a favour. I ask you. Please."

The audience roared at him. He threw up his hands in despair, and waddled quickly back up the aisle.

She had thrown back her black opera-cloak and under it and above it they saw the same form and face they had always loved. Applause was nearly breaking out again, but she hushed it.

"You were always wanting to hear something of Julia Montagu, of her beginnings, of her parentage. I want to tell you to-night about a place, and about myself. I want to tell you about Rathlin Island.

"You may never have heard of Rathlin," she went on. The voice came soft and evenly, and there was a pathetic little smile on her lips. "It is a little green place off the coast of Antrim. It is between Ireland and Scotland. Very green; greener than Ireland, I think. To the left of it are the nine glens of Antrim. To right of it are the Lowlands of Scotland. North of it the sea goes straight to the Pole.

"There are few people in Rathlin—a few hundred fisher-folk; a Free Kirk minister, and The

ANTI-CLIMAX

Campbell of Raghery, as we call it in Gaelic, and his family. The Free Kirk minister, fifteen years ago, was my father, the Reverend Peter Donohu. My name is not Montagu, but Donohu—Sheila Donohu, and" she smiled "I am a real minister's daughter.

"I want now to tell you about The Campbell of Raghery and his six big sons, all called Neil. The Campbell of Raghery is an hereditary title and he is a sort of monarch of the island, feudal lord. The Campbell of my time was a very old man, with a long white beard, very erect and strong, and very fierce. He held to his family customs, and dressed in his saffron kilt and cap with the eagle's feather. Many is the time I've seen him on the cliffs of Raghery, his long beard floating in the breeze, taking snuff, and looking about him like a king. At Christmas time his big sons would be with him, and in the summer, too. There was Neil More and Neil Roe; the big Neil and the red one; there was Neil Donn and Neil Bawn; the brown and the white-haired; there was Neil Duv and Neil Beg; the black-haired Neil and Neil the Little. That was Neil Duv on the screen.

"Neil More and Neil Roe are dead now; they died at sea. Neil Donn is dead, too. He died of

ANTI-CLIMAX

a broken heart over a Frenchwoman, and so is Neil Bawn—he fell down the cliffs of Raghery getting a flower for a child. Neil Duv was the youngest of them all, and he was the one I liked the best. He used to watch me at my plays in the fields along the cliff. He was always very gentle to me. I mind him well——" she broke off for a moment. There was an instant's silence. She blushed gradually; grew embarrassed.

"A lot of men asked me to marry them," she said in low tones. "And I never could. The reason was I loved Neil Duv. I have to tell this," she said in a shamed apology.

"I don't know where I get the strain that made an actress of me," she went on. "Perhaps from the Highland women, perhaps from some French blood that came over with Mary Queen of Scots. But when my father died, the poor, gentle man, there was nothing for me to do in Raghery. I told no one what I wanted to do, but I went to my cousin, Richardson of Belfast, and I told him.

"'A-well,' he said, 'the devil comes after some women, but some women go after the devil. If you change your name—you'll understand me—I'll see you get a chance.' He got me my chance and the rest you know.

ANTI-CLIMAX

"I played in pictures for a while, and at last the time came for this one, and we went to Africa. In a hotel at Tangier whom should I see but Neil Duv Campbell. He recognized me by my picture. He came over.

"'Do you know me, Sheila Donohu?" he said.

"'Do I know the fingers on my right hand, Neil Duv?' I told him. And right before my eyes he was as I had pictured him!" A low, throbbing note crept into her voice—a note of pride. "Tall and lean, sun-bronzed and wind-tanned, with the eagle's eye and the eagle's beak. My heart got low within me. In a minute I'll tell you why.

"He said to me that Neil Beg was dead. He had died in Saigon where they were both going up to Angkor, on a sort of exploring expedition. His father was dead, too, and he was now The Campbell of Raghery. I cried then because of Neil Beg. For Neil Beg was his favourite brother —a wee laughing fellow, with eyes like stars. I was crying when Mr. Foster came in—Mr. Foster the director.

"'Your picture's spoiled!' he groaned. He looked at The Campbell. 'By the Lord Harry, I've got it,' he said. 'You'll do!'

"I told Mr. Foster what a mistake he was making;

ANTI-CLIMAX

that this was The Campbell of Raghery. Mr. Foster didn't know what that meant, but he knew he had committed a solecism. But Neil Duv laughed.

"'Rather than spoil little Sheila's picture,' he said, 'I'll do anything you want me to.' And so he acted for us.

"I noticed he looked queerly at Kenton when he saw him.

"'I think we've met before,' said Neil.

"'I think not, my man!' Kenton answered. But the flash in Neil's eye made him stop that talk.

"I'll tell you now why my heart sank when I saw Neil Duv Campbell. It was because I had promised to marry Roy Kenton. I hate to say this, but I've got to—to make things clear. For a year the man had been asking me to marry him, night and noon and morning—crying, threatening to kill himself. At last, out of sheer weariness, I agreed. I do hate to tell this!" she looked pathetically at the audience.

"The picture was nearly finished when Neil heard of it. He came to me in a white rage.

"'I love you, little Sheila Donohu, body and soul, and I've always loved you, and I love you more than ever now. And not because of me, but

ANTI-CLIMAX

for your sake I'm not going to let you marry this man. Come here, Kenton!'"

Her voice rang out suddenly like a trumpet-call. The audience sat breathless in its seats. Against the white background of the screen she seemed to tower, her shadow lengthening into Titanic proportions.

"'I thought I knew you,' he said to Kenton. 'You were kicked out of the army because your accounts were wrong. You were dropped by your London clubs because you cheated at bridge.' Kenton tried to bluster.

"'Come here, you!' Neil brought in a cringing Levantine Greek. 'This man runs a gambling-house in the Street of the Coppersmiths. Tell me, Georgeopoulos, why did you give this man Kenton credit at your faro table?'

"'Because, *Sidi*,' the Greek replied, 'the man said he was going to marry Miss Montagu, the actress, who was very rich and would give him money.' 'Get out of here!' Neil roared at the actor. 'Get out before I kill you!' and Kenton slunk away."

The audience was stricken dumb for a minute. Then a succession of gasps, a rumble of conversation.

ANTI-CLIMAX

"I went to Neil in the garden that evening where he was sitting smoking, lonely and sad. 'Why are you sad, Neil Duv?' I asked him. 'I'll tell you, little Sheila!' he said. 'Since Bruce came to Ireland, there has always been The Campbell of Raghery, and with me it dies.'"

Her face was rosy, but there was pride shining in her eyes.

"I stole up behind him, and I put my arms about his shoulders. I could feel all his muscles tense suddenly."

She had forgotten the audience entirely. She stood, her hands clasped loosely, her voice lilting like some magnificent barcarolle. She was silent then, as though her thoughts had outrun her tongue.

"We were married then." She paused for an instant, and something hard crept into her voice. "That last scene you saw was taken the morning before. It was then Kenton took his coward's revenge. It was then he smashed that rhinoceros whip across Neil Duv's face. Neil Duv who could have killed him with one hand!

"He will never act again for the movies, will Kenton!" Her voice began to crack like a whip. "When I saw that weal livid across the face of

ANTI-CLIMAX

Neil Duv, of my lover, of my husband, I picked up the whip and lashed it across and across Kenton's face until they tore me from him!"

She stopped, white with passion. A man in the orchestra clapped suddenly, as in savage applause. She took no notice of it. She looked straight at the audience, her eyes filled with tears.

"I came here to-night to see this picture. I came alone, because I wanted to take a sentimental farewell of what I am leaving behind. But when I saw you recoil before the picture of my husband I felt as though I had been stricken in the face." She began to cry suddenly. "And when I saw you pleased when that horrible blow was given him, and he was lying there inert on the sand, I couldn't contain myself." She was shaking now and her voice breaking. She held out her hands. Her tears dropped upon the stage. "It was wrong. It was cruel. You shouldn't, you shouldn't——"

The fat, bald-headed little manager was waddling down the aisle again. Behind him swung a lean figure in a dinner jacket. The manager was pushed aside. With a bound the bronzed, supple figure was on the stage. It might have been a rehearsed kidnapping so deftly was it done. He gathered her up swiftly and strode down the stairs

ANTI-CLIMAX

and up the aisle, her sobs muffled against his shoulder.

"Take me away, Neil! Take me away!" she was crying.

The little manager ran up and down in a frenzy while the audience sat in dumb, stunned silence. At last he caught the eye of the orchestra leader and waved at him furiously. The conductor's baton rapped twice, but the orchestra paid no heed. Only the flautist, by some hazard, obeyed, and from his instrument came a trill, a silver crescendo, that ended in a long strain, dying plaintively, like the notes of some strange, lovely bird.

VI

THE COCK AND BULL STORY OF CAPTAIN BURGOYNE

From Seventy-second Street, if you look northward, and from One Hundred-and-Sixteenth Street, if you look southward, your eye cannot escape the white turrets of the great apartment-house at Ninety-sixth Street and Riverside Drive. Newspaper writers, who have higher ideas for their pens, call it a "caravanserai," and the New Yorker, who after all is a very credulous person, smiles in amused contempt when he happens to think of the Colossus of Rhodes or of the Hanging Gardens of Babylon. He will tell you of the luxuries it contains in each of its one hundred and forty apartments—doors of glass with knobs of crystal; panelled dining-rooms that make the smoky oaken commons halls of Oxford look new and garish; miraculous electrical devices; bathrooms, the luxury of which Roman emperors never knew; cupboards with stained glass outrivalling the windows of the most ornate cathedral; a staff of janitors, hall-boys, telephone operators and the

THE COCK AND BULL STORY

like dressed in red plush and organized like a regiment.

Outside, along the Drive, you may admire the exterior with leisure. It swings toward heaven in a vast mass of white stone like a steam geyser shooting skyward. You see the small, leaded windows like the windows of a Surrey cottage and you see the great French ones, like apertures in the house which the workmen have forgotten to fill. You see turrets and balconies as in a Moorish stronghold; and the huge, latticed iron door, like the entrance to an Old-World castle, and about it all the time there are visible the much-talked-of servitors in red plush—contented, industrious, like the vassals of some great and good lord. Passengers on the steamers watch it on their way up and down the Hudson; people crane their necks to see it from the tops of 'buses. Occasionally a labour agitator stands outside and looks at it with haggard, baleful eyes, and with unspoken curses in the corners of his drawn lips.

It neither bewildered nor irritated Jean Master as he passed into it that September evening. It amused him rather. He preferred, for his own part, that brownstone house on Madison Avenue that another Jean Master, eighty years before, had built with chosen stone and picked mortar, and had welded

THE COCK AND BULL STORY

together with pride and affection. But among the population of Wall Street men and great opera singers, manufacturers and statesmen, that the house contained were his friends, Jan Van Brunt, the Orientalist, and his wife Rita. And as he picked his way across the wonderful mosaic, that cloud of blue and white and pearl grey that only a great artist could have conceived and executed, he found himself smiling in kindness at the love of this couple of which the great apartment-house was witness. They lived there, Master knew, because Van Brunt wanted the most costly home in New York for his bride, and she, uncomfortable as she was in the midst of the light and glitter of it, was happy because to give it to her made him happy.

Dinner was over. A trim French maid, like a character in a musical comedy, had brought coffee in those shell-like gold-inlaid cups that a Mandarin of Macao had given to Jan Van Brunt. Master glanced at the people in the gold-and-red dining-room. By his side, very beautiful and very empty-headed, was the Barbour girl, with her liquid mare's eyes and Futurist hands. Opposite him, talking to Van Brunt himself, was Nadine Scheff, her swarthy Rumanian features and her man's jaw showing up like a menace. In her quiet, effective way, Rita Van

THE COCK AND BULL STORY

Brunt faced the room. A fair-haired Walloon girl, a refugee, from Brussels, played ineptly on the piano, and in a corner of the room, buried in an armchair and talking to De Morganheim, of the Russian Embassy, was Captain Patrick Burgoyne.

"There is something on Burgoyne's mind," said Master to himself, as he saw him knot and unknot his eyebrows, drum his fingers on the edge of the chair and shoot rapid-fire glances at the corner near the open log-fire where Master was dozing luxuriously.

You would never have taken Patrick Burgoyne for a city man, in spite of the somewhat dandified cut of his evening clothes, and his sleek, well-groomed head. There was something about the bronzed, muscular hands, and about the bronzed, gaunt face, with its passive, half-closed eyes, that suggested dank forests and icy mountains and arid, sun-battered plains. You always had the idea, from the very stillness of the man, that he would rise suddenly to the full height of his lean six feet and smash at you with paralyzing quickness. In various zoological gardens you will find queer beasts from Africa and Sumatra and Tibet in iron cages with donation-cards on the outside bearing the name of Captain Patrick Burgoyne. In recondite journals that appear

THE COCK AND BULL STORY

but twice a year, and in the Transactions of obscure but extremely learned societies, you will find his signature at the bottom of ethnological and geographical papers. In the first editions of metropolitan dailies, when news is very scarce, a paragraph may be found reporting that the King of Sweden has made Burgoyne a Knight of the Polar Star, or that the Royal Society has given him a medal. If you want an opinion of his merits as an explorer and a hunter you will have to ask Sven Hedin, or Vilhjalmur Stefansson, or Sir Harry Browne. The New York public knows of him as a romantic figure appearing out of Africa or Tibet or Polynesia, playing some huge and unconscious joke, and disappearing again. They remember with glee how an Institute expedition returning from Africa had told of a new and wonderful mammal called the liapoh, which only they had seen, and which could not be brought back alive. New York was impressed until, fifteen days later, Burgoyne, returning on another boat, led a queer, goat-like, striped little animal into a taxicab and drove up with it, without saying a word, to the Bronx Zoo. They remember how a Smithsonian expedition had climbed to the highest peak in the Hindu-Kush, only to find there a silver cigarette-case with the initials "P.B." They remember how

THE COCK AND BULL STORY

when a manuscript of Mahmoud-el-Afghani, the Pushtu poet, had been discovered, and three universities had failed to translate it becomingly, Burgoyne had it done by his personal attendant who happened to be a famous Turkoman Sufi, a pilgrim to Mecca, and a doctor of Amsterdam University. And New York laughed quietly. It appreciated a man who could do those things.

Burgoyne looked impatiently across the room toward Master. He fidgeted in his chair. He leaned over quickly toward the Russian *attaché*.

"You will have to excuse me, Vassili Petrovitch," Master heard him apologize in his deep, humming tone. "There is something important I want to say to my friend Jean Master."

He strode across the room with that extraordinary step of his, that swing upward from the ball of the foot which the Galla tribesman uses. He might have been stepping over a treacherous veldt instead of over a grey-and-blue Chinese rug. He let himself noiselessly into a chair beside Master, who looked at his corrugated brow with deep amusement.

"What's on your mind, Patrick?" he asked grimly. "What's worrying your little brain?"

The explorer squared his jaw and knitted his brows. "Know the Greek quarter here, Master?"

THE COCK AND BULL STORY

he demanded abruptly in his deep baritone. "Know where the Greeks live?"

"One of the most interesting quarters in New York City," Master began in the sing-song of a professional guide, "is the Greek quarter. From Fortieth Street southward along Sixth Avenue it extends to Thirty-third Street. Here one may see the sons of the sunny south at work and at leisure—making their cigarettes in the windows, running employment agencies, pool-parlours, boot-black stands, peanut furnaces, and restaurants. It is one of the baffling psychological problems of our time, how this people, descended as they are from the Spartans of old——"

"Stop fooling," Burgoyne warned. "I'm serious. Sixth Avenue won't do. Where else do they live?"

"A few in the Bronx; a few in Harlem; a few everywhere, but they accumulate mostly in Sixth Avenue—that is, the gregarious ones."

"Did you ever hear of any very famous Greek woman in New York?" the explorer continued. "Vaudeville artist, actress, singer—anything like that?"

"I never did. I don't think there is any one," Master answered.

"Ever hear of any big house owned by a Greek,

THE COCK AND BULL STORY

or a Greek woman, in New York, very luxurious, very ornate?"

"No." Master looked at him in wonder. "I never did. And if there were such a thing I should have known of it."

Burgoyne's jaw protruded again. His eyes half closed.

"Look here, Patrick," Master exploded, "if there's anything on your mind, get it off quickly. Let's have the story and we'll see what we can do about it. Come on. Unburden yourself to your little Uncle Jean."

"Ever hear me speak of Domenico Varras?" Burgoyne asked.

"Never." Master shook his head.

"I don't suppose you did. I don't like to talk about unpleasant subjects. Domenico Varras was one of the most thorough-paced scoundrels in the Old or the New Worlds, and Domenico Varras is dead."

He looked at his finger-tips savagely, trying to concentrate his thoughts. Master, who had heard him tell his stories before, kept very silent.

"He was a very heavy, short man," Burgoyne went on, "with a head that was as round as a coin, except where it was broken by the features of the

THE COCK AND BULL STORY

face. He was about five-foot-four and weighed two hundred and fifty pounds, all heavy bone and muscle. His skin was as dark as a mulatto's. He had an immense nose, hooked like a scimitar, and little black eyes, with eyebrows like another man's moustaches. He walked very heavily and painfully, like a Spanish peasant. And he invariably was dressed, whether it was in the middle of Africa or on top of the Hindu-Kush, in a sack suit of blue serge, with a heavy, gold chain across his vest and a heavy bone charm attached to the chain. Am I boring you?"

"Go ahead, for heaven's sake," Master answered.

"The first time I met Domenico Varras was in Canton in 1899. He was then financing a mosquito fleet of Chinese pirates in the Yellow Sea. The Allied Powers cleaned him out of that. The second time I met him was 1904. He was doing a little bit of slaving in Uganda. In 1907 he was raiding the Belgian Congo for rubber and tusks. Leopold got him, and instead of shooting him without mercy, they imprisoned him at Leopoldville. Of course he got out. It cost him every penny he had in the world, but he got away. I met him on the quay in Sydney, Australia, in 1911, and by George! the man had even pawned his stiletto—and when a Neapolitan does that!"

THE COCK AND BULL STORY

Burgoyne smiled to himself gently, and knocked the tip off his cigarette. " He said he was going to Samoa and he went."

The explorer slapped his knee impatiently and swung around to Master. "The queer thing about it was," he snapped, "that in his own profession Varras had no peer. He was one of the most wonderful church decorators in the world—Varras could do things with mosaic that other men could not do with paint and brushes. He was wonderful. But he was inherently bad. He would only work in mosaic when he could do nothing else—when there wasn't a crime in sight and he was down to his last penny.

"I'll tell you another queer thing about him, *à propos* of nothing at all: He was intensely religious and intensely superstitious about it. He would touch nothing in a church. A friar might pass along the road carrying the King of Spain's diamonds, and Varras would genuflect and let him pass by. If you understand what I mean, it was *tabu* on him, as the Polynesians say, not to commit a crime involving anything religious. He mustn't do that, do you see? That was his limitation."

Burgoyne looked into the log fire. He seemed to have forgotten Master—another peculiarity of

THE COCK AND BULL STORY

Burgoyne's, a peculiarity engendered in the blue African nights.

"Well, where's the story?" Master asked petulantly, after three minutes' silence. "What did he die of, and what's all this about the Greek woman?"

"Here it is," Burgoyne continued: "Early this year, 1916, Varras turned up in Port Said. He had gone, he said, from Samoa to New York. In New York, after a while, he had to hide himself—you'll know why in a minute. He managed to sneak over on a Levantine freighter, to look for an Arab physician. He was a leper. Most acute form. Two days after landing he died. I hate to think of even Domenico Varras going out that way, though heaven knows after the things he did in his life a dog's death in a ditch was too good for him."

"Ugh!" Master shuddered.

"You're right," Burgoyne nodded. "Let's forget it. Here's the part you want to hear about the Greek woman: Hassan Mansur-el-Arabi, the old sheik from Bagdad, told it to me in Cairo, on the terrace of Shepheard's Hotel. There was something on Varras' mind when he was dying, something he wanted to say, and he told it to the Syrian inn-keeper. It travelled about for a while before it came to Hassan. Varras said this: 'I was having no luck, and besides,

THE COCK AND BULL STORY

I was becoming afraid of him, so I buried him in the house we were building in New York for the Greek woman, where the sun was rising, between the two silver torches set in the walls.' There you have it."

"What did you make of it?" Master asked calmly.

"I didn't make much of it," Burgoyne puzzled. "I could only make out what he said. He buried something, or someone, in a house in New York, on which he was at work—he must have been penniless or he would not have been working—that was being built for a Greek client. He buried this, or him, in the eastern part of the building, 'where the sun was rising,' between two silver torches. That's the reason I asked about the ornate house—those silver torches!"

"He was a specialist in mosaic work, you said," Master interrupted.

"He was an artist in it," replied Burgoyne.

"About what time was he in America?"

"Let me see," the explorer reflected. "He died early this year. The particularly malignant form of leprosy he had must have been of two years' standing. He couldn't have got into America if it had been noticeable, so he was probably at work here late in 19—— and early in 19——."

THE COCK AND BULL STORY

"The year this house was finished," Master mentioned, casually. He threw back his head and looked at the ceiling. Suddenly he burst in a rapid carillon of laughter, like a baritone scale being rung in a belfry. Amusement poured from his lips and eyes like bubbles flowing over the neck of a wine-bottle.

"What the mischief are you laughing at?" Burgoyne demanded savagely.

"Not at you, my dear fellow, not at you," he grinned. "Listen, Rita. Tell me something, will you?"

Van Brunt's wife slipped across the room in a shimmer of pink silk. She looked at him amusedly out of the corners of her grey eyes.

"What is the name of this—'caravanserai,' I think is the term?" Master inquired. "What do they call this apartment-house?"

"Why! The 'Aspasia,'" she answered.

"'The house of the Greek woman,'" Master turned to Burgoyne with a smile. "And tell me, Rita, are there any silver torches about?"

"Not silver," she laughed. "Luxury doesn't extend quite that far as yet! But down in the hall there are two very gorgeous wall-lamps, one on each side of the passage, fashioned like torches. They are not silver, though—they are merely aluminum."

THE COCK AND BULL STORY

"Good enough for the untutored mind," Master commented. "There's your riddle solved, Patrick."

"But the rising sun, man!" Burgoyne snapped out. "'Where the sun is rising,' how do you explain that?"

"Rita," Master began again easily, "what is the pattern of the mosaic in the hall?"

"Oh, that!" she began warmly. "I'm very enthusiastic about that. It is a picture of dawn. Heavy pearl clouds and a blue sky, and a great red sun just suggesting itself among them. It's one of the most wonderful pieces of mosaic in the world and done by a practically unknown Italian to whom Mr. Epstein gave the chance because he was helplessly poor and ill. He disappeared after it was finished. Barro, I think, the name was."

"Varras," corrected Master. "Domenico Varras."

Burgoyne rose to his six feet with a bound. His jaw squared.

"I'm going to have that mosaic up," he announced calmly.

"You can't!" Rita Van Brunt objected. "You're mad, both of you."

"We're not mad," Master smiled tauntingly, "and moreover, we are going to have that mosaic up. Who owns the house?"

THE COCK AND BULL STORY

"Mr. Epstein over there," she nodded. "The man who sat beside you at dinner."

Across the room, where she motioned, they saw Epstein, the owner of the building, a small dapper Jew, with the build and features of an Oriental Napoleon. As Burgoyne and he crossed the room, Master noticed the man's bulldog jaw and soft, lustrous, woman's eyes. A poet, he judged, more than a great merchant, a man who conducted a huge business for the adventure there was in it, and who accumulated money for the romance of power.

"Mr. Epstein," Burgoyne began bluntly, "I'm going to have up your mosaic——"

"Pardon me, Patrick, pardon me." Master looked at him with an expression of disgust. "We would like your permission, Mr. Epstein, to remove a part of the mosaic in the hall. We believe there is something hidden there. Do you mind?"

Epstein looked at Burgoyne with a grin. "Any friend of this family's," he answered with the gallantry of an emperor, "may place dynamite under the house if he wants. He may take the house away with him. He may sell it and pocket the cash. Go ahead and dig anywhere you want to. The hall-boys will get you picks and a shovel."

They moved towards the door with a word of

THE COCK AND BULL STORY

thanks. Rita Van Brunt caught at Master's arm. "Wait till I get a wrap," she said excitedly. "I'm coming too."

She started suddenly when she saw that Master's face had become grey and haggard like a man's face at the dawn when he has not slept overnight. The corners of his mouth were drawn tight and through the tensed veins on his forehead the blood could be seen to pulse in nervous, staccato bounds.

"What's wrong, Jean?" she asked. "What's the matter? Tell me quickly."

"I don't know what wrong," Master replied grimly. "And I should hate to tell you what I'm afraid of, but you mustn't come, Rita, you mustn't come."

They slipped out of the door and down the one flight of stairs to the hall, scorning the elevator. At the turn in the stairs Burgoyne caught Master by the wrist.

"What are you afraid of?" he asked tersely.

Master's teeth chattered with horror. Colour ebbed and flowed in his face like a wave on a shore. His hands closed until the knuckles showed like pieces of white marble. "You remember," he stammered, "he was afraid, and there was no luck, and he buried him——"

"Well?" the explorer snapped.

THE COCK AND BULL STORY

"Don't you see? Oh, I feel ill. Let me catch the banister. Don't you know the superstition of the masons that a man must die before a house or a bridge will stand? Don't you know that the master-builders used to make, and make still, for all you and I know, a human sacrifice that a spirit may guard the place? Great heavens! It's down there. It's down there, and I'm afraid."

"We've got to see," said Burgoyne. But even his voice was shaky and weak.

They dipped into the garish hall, where tall mirrors rose as in a palace, where light radiated from the huge candelabrum above, and from the two silver torches at the sides. In front of them, stretching like a landscape, was the great miracle of colour in mosaic. Blue ebbed into grey, and the grey was tinged with mauve. Great clouds were massed like the pearly smoke of furze bushes. The pearl became pink and the pink was tinged with scarlet. High in the blue was the iridescent silver shimmer of the morning star, while toward the wall the sun peeked in a scarlet haze.

"Get a pick and shovel," said Burgoyne to the hall-boy.

Outside, as Master looked, dazed and ill, Riverside Drive flowed like a river. Automobiles spun along

THE COCK AND BULL STORY

like balls. The black road-bed shone like polished carbon, and the white lights of the arc-lamps showed fiercely against it, like the flash of spangles on a dark gown. White lights licked like clouds across the surface of the river, and trees showed hazily like shadows. Across the river the Fort Lee boat trundled in a blaze of light, steadily, unimaginatively, as it were, like a stout peasant woman going to market. Hazily still, but completely, Master took in all the details of what was going on in the hall—the grinning faces of the hall-boys, the bringing of pick and shovel, and a piece of sacking on which to place the tiny pieces of marble. It jarred him that all this every-day life should go on about him, the rolling motors, the grinning servants, the tooting ferry, when he felt they were about to unearth the evidence of horrible, unspeakable crimes. Suddenly he saw that a hall-boy had raised the pick a couple of feet from the ground in order to strike. "In the name of heaven! Dig!" Master cried involuntarily.

Little pictures ran through his mind—queer macabre dances of building tradition. He saw the laying of the stone and the rising of the wall; arches taking shape and beauty; turrets rounding; the work finished and the last touch to be made—the spirit that must guard the masons' work. He saw vaguely

THE COCK AND BULL STORY

the terrible Ritual of the Artificers, the trap, the victim, the shut-off cry, the horrible silence. It had been done for Solomon's Temple, so they say. It had been done for the Moorish palaces of Granada. Even the brown-tonsured Brothers, if it can be believed, forgot their Christian faith while they sacrificed that their monasteries might stand while grass grew and water ran. But in New York! In 19———! The hall-boy straightened himself.

"There's something here," he said.

With a few deft scoops of his hands he uncovered a parcel of rough sacking, not taller than a man's forearm and not broader than a man's head. Master laughed, weak as he was from the strain. "What an ass I am!" he bellowed. "I was afraid. I thought it was a dead man."

Burgoyne did not laugh. He looked at the package with his set jaw and his everlasting knitted brows. "I'm afraid of no man," he said slowly, "living or dead—but I'm afraid of what's in that packet. Get me a pair of automobile gloves."

He pulled them on with a brusque gesture and leaning down whipped off the layer of sacking. There was another cover of green flannel that once had been a man's shirt. He held something brown and white in his hands.

THE COCK AND BULL STORY

"Ah, I thought as much," he said.

It was a brown statue, Master saw, a wonderful, finely carved thing of brown wood and silver, and pathetically deformed. The legs were swollen and the silver work suggested minute and glistening scales. Here and there was a flash of green emerald and microscopic pearls like dew-drops. The eyes were moonstones with the flash of red. Two shrimps of arms were held out in an attitude of appeal. There was something horrible in the deformities of the statue, but passing the tragic horror of it was the poignant, dignified appeal, the call for charity and understanding. Master took a step forward to take it from Burgoyne.

"Keep away," the explorer snapped. "Keep away. Don't touch it."

"What is it?" Master asked.

"It is Lanilahi, the leper-god of Polynesia. The mad fool! He had to steal it."

"You think that's why he died," Master stammered, "that way?"

"I know it," said Burgoyne.

He turned to the astounded hall-boy with a sudden swing of his shoulders. "Put on a pair of gloves," he directed, "and take those rags and burn them in the furnace. Burn them to ashes, do you hear? Come on, Master."

THE COCK AND BULL STORY

He stepped out of the hall into the soft night on the Drive. He swung across the roadway, and walked down the steps that lead to the shrubbery between Drive and river. He walked unhesitatingly like a man who has taken a right decision.

"I say," Master broke in as he hurried after him, "he never touched anything connected with religion, didn't you tell me?"

"Never, until the last time," Burgoyne answered grimly.

"He must have known it," Master continued. "He broke his limitation."

"He broke his *tabu*," Burgoyne nodded.

They had reached the edge of the water now. Burgoyne drew his right arm back like a discus thrower. He sent the idol through the air into the river in a long, swinging curve. They heard it splash musically.

"You should not have done that, Burgoyne," Master objected with a twinge of conscience. "You should have turned it over to the health authorities. Somebody will pick it up when it drifts ashore."

"It won't drift ashore."

"Why won't it?"

"Because it's on its way back to Samoa," said Captain Patrick Burgoyne.

VII

THE EVIL MEN DO

There is a preachment of William Shakespeare—in his tragedy of *Julius Cæsar* you will find it—that the evil that men do lives after them; the good is oft interred with their bones. And when I read that, I think always of Ghiyathuddin Abulfatti Omar bin Ibrahim al-Khayyám of Nishapur, whom we call familiarly "old Khayyám."

"The paragon of scientists", his contemporaries called him, who, because he was head and shoulders above the astronomers of his time, was appointed by Malik, the great Shah, to the observatory royal at Merv. There he passed away his time charting the heavens, compiling those wonderful tables of his called *Zij*. There he produced his great calendar, rivalling that of Gregory the Pope. There he rebuked Euclid of Alexandria, the subtle geometrist, for the laxness of his definitions. There, pondering by night, he wrote his treatise on algebra, laying the foundations of the binomial theorem that four centuries later our Newton perfected.

THE EVIL MEN DO

And in the intervals of that great work of pricking out on the blue chart of the sky the lesser and the greater constellations, the fixed and the wandering stars; of grasping from the current of possibilities the exactitudes of science; of putting a halter on the running year, apportioning into days and weeks and seasons the period of the peach blossoms and the days of snow, in this work he sought distraction in the making of rubais, revolting against the fanatical mysticism of the Sufis of his day, much as a banker of our times might dabble in art, or a statesman amuse himself by the writing of nonsensical limericks.

And that is what we remember to-day of Omar al-Khayyám of Nishapur in Khorassan; not the treatise on the fluxional calculus, or the tables called *Zij*, or the *Tarikh-i-Makik-Shahi*, his great calendar, but the quatrains of wine and flowers translated for us in luscious, seductive rhyme, mouthed by slightly bibulous men in their cups, quoted of frail women, a revelation and a gospel to the fleshy opportunists of our day. "There with a loaf of bread beneath the bough," they carol, "a flask of wine, a book of verse, and Thou!" "Oh Thou Who didst with pitfall and with gin——" they whine. "Ah, take the cash in hand and waive the rest," they quote with their cynical leer, "nor heed the rumble of a distant drum!"

THE EVIL MEN DO

"Khayyám," wrote the great scientist in his old age—when he had seen the fame his verses were attaining and was tasting the contempt of his bardic associates:

> "Khayyám, who stitched the tents of science,
> Has fallen in grief's furnace and been suddenly burned.
> The shears of Fate have cut the tent-ropes of his life,
> And the broker of Hope has sold him for nothing!"

I

Now, when Peter L'hommedieu Mongel, fat in the body, full in the beard, died in Fall River in 1911, I think nobody, and certainly not his son, was overcome with grief at the loss of him. The sterling virtues of the ancient Huguenot strain which had produced that man had ossified in him into an intense hardness, a crude materialism. The cautious economy of his Gallic forbears had in him become a manner of hypocritical rapacity. He was bluff and hearty, was old Peter, with a word for everyone, but his laughing manner and his great voice rang somehow hollowly, and children ran from him when he approached them to demand how they were succeeding at school, or any of the thousand bantering questions which the old gentlemen of a bygone time used to put to the little ones in the streets. Even the shrewd Hebrew traders felt contempt for his methods.

"Money is a good thing," MacAllister, the Scotch designer at Hoffman's used to philosophize. "It takes away the troubles of life, enabling a man to spend a proper amount of time in the saving of his soul; but the way that the Frenchman, Mongel, goes after money is unco disagreeable to me."

He might have been pardoned for his rapacity, had he had any worthy object in view; but the man had none. It was his pleasure and his pride that he ground the last cent of profit possible out of the operatives in his mills. At his home he was liberal in the keeping of his table. He liked a good meal and he had an eye for a pretty woman. On one of his trips to Dijon and to Switzerland he had brought back a pretty French wife, who had been a minor actress at the Odéon. She died two years after, having given him a son, John L'hommedieu Mongel. She died, drowned in that roaring personality as a thin glass might be shattered in the crash of a cataract.

Thus much of Peter, the old mill-owner. Thus much and little more. To his son he paid little attention, treating him more in the nature of some innocuous pet about the house, sending him to school, giving

THE EVIL MEN DO

him a liberal allowance, using him occasionally as an appurtenance to his own vast vanity.

A very queer figure this man Mongel seems to me, very queer for a Frenchman. He paid more attention to his occasional amours than to the son who was to perpetuate his name and keep intact the family fortune. Another man would have seen to it that the boy had a regular training in the business. Not so old Mongel.

"This is a one man business, and I am the one man, do you see?" he laughed. "My little one, you have not my brains nor my personality; you cannot succeed. When I am gone, you can have it, for then I will have no more need for it. Wine it, gamble it, throw it away. What do I care? All things end with death. I know it, for I have studied the affair."

And so he passed through life, with his fat paunch and his full beard, his loud laughter and his hard eyes, his heavy malacca cane and his pot hat, very like a Juggernaut. A sensual man, selfish, overbearing, damned sententious. Unregretted, he died.

II

I hear little of John Mongel when at school, and that little, indefinite. He seems to remain in the memories of his masters as a personality, not as a student. A gay, laughing boy, given overmuch to practical jokes and to the compounding of queer words to express things and men. Always in the forefront, inclined to unconscious acting, bubbling like a charged wine.

"He seemed to have saved up all his gaiety at home," the old Latin master remembers, "and to have discharged it here. As a student, particularly with his Cæsar—" But his Cæsar interests me as little as it did Mongel; Cæsar, the dry, baldheaded warrior continually going into winter quarters.

The vacations in Fall River were silent, introspective times. He would wander about the hustling, purposeful town, that is like some stripped, labouring giant, covered with the grime of work. Down by the river the great factories hummed like one unanimous, titanic loom. The empty streets around were like some silent reproach to drones, and at noontime and in the evening they belched forth great quantities of workers, like swarming bees. A huddled, bent population, they entered with the greyness of dawn and emerged with the close of day.

"They seem to ask for nothing," the boy wondered. It was one of the rare times he spoke aloud to his father those secret thoughts of his.

THE EVIL MEN DO

"Consider the silkworm, my son, an intelligent beast. It spins for no master, asking only to work. Shall human beings, then, be less intelligent than the little dumb animal?"

At college the memory of the lad is much more vivid; because he was interested in every living thing, attracted by everything that had animation, from a flower by the wayside to a workman at the loom. His interest swerved from the clear-cut mathematical things to the vague values of human life and labour.

"Very naturally," someone said, "seeing that he was prospective owner of one of the biggest properties in New England."

No! There was very little of his father in John Mongel. I can see his mother, the little French actress, who had known poverty and the strictness of labour, brooding over the Mongel fortune in those months before the boy was born, fiercely antagonistic to the selfishness of the boy's father; revolting against the man's rapacity; cut to the quick by his cynicism.

But at any rate, at college, John Mongel threw himself with all his Gallic impetuous quality into the study of the probabilities of human action in economic matters. The dry fabric of the economic formulæ—Gresham's law, value-in-use, value-in-exchange, the phenomenon of diminishing returns—took fire in his imagination and blazed into a pageantry of commerce that outranked the Spanish conquests for romance. Along the green New England seaboard he could visualize the clipper ships setting out under a cloud of sail for the Indies and for China and for Frisco Bay. Westward came the armies of labour, heavy-moving, inexorable, armed with the hammer and the compass and the rule. Great looms purred and there was the roaring of gigantic furnaces. From the beds of bleak rivers red gold was plucked, and from repellent-looking ore shining battleships and caravans of trains took material and shape. They looted the bosom of the earth for the stones which builded towers high as the dome that Noe's sons reared at Babel of Shinar. Sailors adventured to the outer seas, and in changing houses labour was paid in clinking yellow counters. A great fabric. A great dream.

Seething with the dream inside him—it was impossible for him to keep it to himself—he talked of it to his professors. They blinked at him solemnly and talked of material and immaterial production and of consumptive and productive capital. They disliked to see the young paw the air, but they meant well. There is that to be said for them.

THE EVIL MEN DO

He talked to the young fanatics of his college. They rebuked him, speaking with the tongues of men and angels.

"What you are talking of is mercantile speculation," they decided, "which is only gambling. Mark now," they warmed up, "how the poor man is oppressed while the rich are allowed iniquity. The gaming tables of the poor man are closed by law, while the Stock Exchange——"

"That be damned!" Mongel told them straight. His hard Latin logic stuck to him through all his dreams.

To his father he made one mention of his symphony of labour. One, and only one.

"It is very deep," the old man declared. "But I have studied the affair and I have solved it. The less money you give to the workers, the more you have for yourself. *Voila!*"

There seemed to be one person who understood him, who saw the rainbow-coloured vision of his dream, and lived it with him, and translated it into practical currency, and that was Eleanor Godley.

THE EVIL MEN DO

III

I wish you could see Eleanor Godley as I see her, a tall girl, slim as a boy, with a bosom almost epicene. A face like the face of a marble statue, long, clear-cut, regular. A flurry of black hair that stands out about her head like an aureole. Keen, large, black eyes that seem to be always studying you, weighing your worth, then throwing you aside as useless. I can conceive of no slight or evil man standing that gaze unabashed. All spirit she seems to be, live, immortal spirit. I should not be surprised to meet Eleanor at dark of night, floating whitely above the earth, a tongue of flame in her hair . . . I see her as a drawn sword.

When Eleanor's father, old Hezekiah Godley, seceding from the shipbuilding colony of the Tyne, came westward toward America, there followed him a sufficient quota of his skilled workers to give him in New Bedford a fair start among his competitors. Old "Quake-in-the-presence-of-the-Lord" Godley, his men called him in sympathetic contempt for his kindly Friend's faith; but at a word from him they would have wrecked a township or captured an

THE EVIL MEN DO

armed force—these rough Tyne workers and the terrible shipwrights from Belfast.

Old Godley is gone now, and the clanging slips where his workers laboured with hammer and plane are owned by a silent man with a close New England mouth, and his name is forgotten, but his principles still live in that tall daughter of his. The gentle Quaker spirit is not hers, but the energy of a Crusader, tempered by a good common sense. The thing he called charity to every man she sees as fair play, and where old Godley would have melted at the sight of a sick child, giving it every attention because of Christian kindness, she would do so for the reason that the child had a right to life and protection.

"You are not going to become a new woman, Eleanor?" her mother would say to her, a frail little lady in Quaker grey and cap and cuffs.

"I am not a new woman, dearest," the girl answered her kindly. "I am only all woman, and the sickly thing, and the oppressed thing shall always have love and protection from me."

It was at the house of her cousins in Fall River, Richardsons the linen people, that she met John Mongel. There was not a family in the manufacturing

THE EVIL MEN DO

town that cared for the elder Mongel, but there was not a family that did not welcome the younger. He looked so lonely, so out of place with the cynical father; and besides, with his coming into a house an air of jollity and freedom entered, as if more windows were thrown open and more lights switched on.

They liked to see him come in, spick and span, as though fresh from a valet's hands, smiling lustrously, his curly head shimmering, his air of "Now, I am here, let the band play and the mayor read the address!" There was a great honesty in his handshake to the men, and even toward the grandmothers of seventy and over he gave the impression of restrained but passionate admiration, for which they adored him.

The first time Eleanor Godley saw him was at a dance at a country club where, in a corner, Mongel was strumming a ukulele, decked out with festooned ribbons, and giving a ludicrous imitation of the buxom Toots Paka in a Hula dance. Her uncle Leonard wanted her to meet the boy. Her lips curled.

"That wretched little buffoon!"

"Yes, exactly, Eleanor," her uncle said with a queer smile, "that wretched little buffoon!" The uncle

THE EVIL MEN DO

was chairman of a big commerce commission and had little time for buffoons either.

Those weighing, probing eyes of hers studied him from head to toe, and there was no abashedness in his expression, but a great frankness. Behind that laughing smile she seemed to feel something and, conquered, she smiled back at him.

It was not very long afterward that she descended on him in righteous anger. Her knowledge of Fall River showed her the bent, broken population of the Mongel mills; the hacking coughs of the operatives in the desiccating room where the raw silk is proven for moisture; the crooked backs from the looms; the pale-faced children who worked as throwsters. There was an air of hidden infamy about it all, the look of a chain gang, the broken despondency of thralls in a feudal system.

"Why don't you do something about it?" she asked. "Or don't you care?" she flared out angrily.

"Do I care?" he riposted at her, as angry as she. His voice dropped. "I care very much, but I can do nothing, nothing much, until——"

"Until your father's dead, you mean," she put it bluntly. "And then?"

"And then, by God!" he swore, unwitting of

anything but his enthusiasm, "and then there'll be a change."

Archibald MacKenzie, manager of the mills, will never cease recounting the history of the day when John Mongel took charge. "'Come in here, MacKenzie,' he says to me, 'come in here and sit down and answer my questions!' And the voice of him was like a trumpet, and my heart went pit-a-pat. Och, aye, pit-a-pat!"

He was sitting at his father's desk. All the windows were open for the first time in years.

"Roughly, how much money are we making a year?" he asked. "Oh, as much as that? Now, MacKenzie, nobody liked my father's method of business, and I least of all. Now what changes are we going to make?"

"We might raise the wages," the Scotchman suggested cautiously.

"We'll certainly do that," Mongel agreed. "How much?"

"So help me God, Mr. John," MacKenzie blurted out. "You might give them twenty-five per cent. and you'd only be making up a little for what they'd lost under the old man."

Mongel played with a paper-cutter on the desk. He looked up finally.

THE EVIL MEN DO

"We'll give them ten," he decided. The Scotsman's face fell. "Don't be worried, MacKenzie. I've got something else I want to do. In the first place, I'm going to organize a guild in this mill and insure them against accident, illness and old age. I'm going this very day——" and he went swiftly into details that made the old manager gasp.

"It's never been done before," old Archibald protested.

"I don't care a tinker's curse about what's been done before."

I don't think the other mill-owners of Fall River were very keen for Mongel's ideas. At first they pooh-poohed them, considering them the experiments of an enthusiastic boy.

"He'll get over it," they prophesied. "In a year or two he'll get sense, and then, by Jove! watch him. Blood will out. The old man will turn up in him yet."

I think it was the enthusiasm of Eleanor Godley that helped spur him on to fresher efforts, made him plunge, not recklessly but with cautious Latin logic, into experiments that have since made industrial history; you can look them up in the dry reading of the industrial reviews, and in the reports of labour commissions. There were many things he owed Eleanor in those days. He did not know it.

"But some day he will," she smiled to herself wisely. She could suggest a thing subtly, very subtly.

"Do you feel any real responsibility for your workmen?" she would ask him.

"Of course I do," he would protest indignantly. "Haven't I got a social service bureau, and that run efficiently?"

"Not so efficiently," she suggested. "You've got a lot of married women working with their husbands for you. Now in case of maternity——" she wavered.

"By George, that's so!" he exploded. "An Endowment of Maternity experiment. It would work, I think. At least, if I lost on it, I'd make up somewhere else."

But he lost nothing. At the end of the year he saw that spacing conditions over time his mills would bring in more than they did under his father's regime. He stood up and stretched his arms.

"MacKenzie," he directed, "you're going to run this place as efficiently as I did or lose your job. I'm going away for a long, long holiday. You'll be lucky if you see me once a month."

THE EVIL MEN DO

To Eleanor Godley he recounted the success of the year's work. There was something behind her glance. She studied him keenly.

"Are you going to enlarge the business?"

"The business, as it stands now, is of a nice size, workable but not clumsy. It can run by itself, being wound up once a month."

"And the rest of the month?"

"My dear girl," he told her with mock seriousness. "I once had a reputation as a humorist. Humour is a rare gift. There is little of it in the world."

"Yes?"

"If I stay any longer working in that atmosphere of reform, I shall end eventually by dressing in black, and growing whiskers."

"I understand," she smiled.

"You follow me. Well then, I have decided from this time forward to give New York a treat." And he said good-bye.

"He is young," she thought, "and with his father, life has been for him a continual repression. He needs it. But he will come back," she thought proudly. "He will come back to me!"

THE EVIL MEN DO

IV

She tossed the paper aside with a look of disgust, and her fine nostrils dilated and her slender bosom rose and sank. An instant later, though, she picked it up. The thing had a repulsive attraction for her. She wanted to burn it in the fire, but she read the offending paragraph again:

"The Wainwright-Todds have, it is rumoured, begun a libel suit against John L'hommedieu Mongel for the little sketch he wrote and put on, aided by Sappho Buchanan, at a garden party given by a prominent hostess in Westchester this summer. They allege that the representation was a burlesque of their marital and temperamental troubles. Sappho Buchanan will be remembered as the heroine of many escapades of the Smart Set during the last four seasons. Her last appearance as the Queen of the Shimmy at the Fakirs' Ball roused considerable comment. John L'hommedieu Mongel is the accredited merry-Andrew of metropolitan society. It is safe to assume that the Wainwright-Todd suit will be withdrawn and the jocund John and the Siren Sappho allowed to go their merry way unhindered. New York society threatens with ostracism any attempt to curtail the activities of its pet Punchinello."

She walked over to the window of her guest room at the Richardsons. In the distance, Fall River lay swarming with industry as a hive might with bees.

THE EVIL MEN DO

Faintly, straining her eyes, she imagined she could see the Mongel mills, square, clean, powerful, like some well-organized, well-captained fortress of labour.

"Pet Punchinello!"

Only a few days ago she had been down there. Already she had seen the great change in the workers. No longer in their faces was the empty, sullen look of an ox treading a mill, the hopeless expression that regards life as a difficult road to a vacant nowhere, to a nepenthe from the pain of work. In their faces self-respect showed, and will, and power. And John Mongel had done that.

She had seen him, three scant months ago, seated in his office with his lieutenants about him—himself dapper, immaculate, smiling, with his dark eyes shining with enthusiasm.

"The upshot of it all is," Mongel had told them, "I'm going to put in the eight-hour day."

"There's a lot of things I approve in what you're doing, Master John," old MacKenzie had typically objected. "Oh, man, ay! I do approve them, but there's a limit."

"There's a limit, but I haven't reached it yet, MacKenzie," Mongel had told him. "There's one rule in these factories, and that's fair play.

THE EVIL MEN DO

I do a lot for the workmen; I expect them to pay me in kind. A slacker has no place here; out he must go! And besides, MacKenzie, I'm going to get the best operatives in the country, the steadiest work, the most concentrated work. The output will be all right, don't you worry, MacKenzie. Study the curve of intensive productivity this year and see if I'm wrong."

He had been wrong in several things, for not all experiments can be successful, but by and large he was right.

"Fire; vision; shrewdness," she thought. "And yet New York's pet Punchinello!"

She looked, as she gazed out through the window, her nostrils quivering, her left hand on her bosom, her right gripping the printed scurrility as though throttling a reptile, like some vision of indignant contempt. Her eyes might have blasted New York's drones had they looked into them. They were half closed now and the long-range anger went from them and something short and stabbing replaced it, like the cracking of whips. She was thinking of a conversation with her uncle Leonard, the commercial expert. He had been talking of the red menace in the North-west.

"The most lawless guerillas in the world," he

THE EVIL MEN DO

had pronounced them. "Selfish! Ruthless! Preachers of sabotage! They respect no stake in the land because they have got nothing themselves. A jail is luxury to them. They are irresponsible. And it is a doctrine of irresponsibility that appeals to the overworked, underpaid workmen. Once let them flirt with that pack, and they take to the woods. And it's spreading, Eleanor, it's spreading."

"What is the answer, Uncle Leonard?" she asked, cleaving straight to the root.

"The answer is John L'hommedieu Mongel, and a host of men of his kind. The men who organize, equip, arm the loyalty of labour to commerce against the drunken insurrectionists. Our John Mongel is like a great strategist against a horde of sansculottes!"

"Pet Punchinello!"

She sank down in her chair, slowly, and the fierce and throbbing anger that was like the throbbing of drums left her and a sort of keen pain came into her heart, like the lonely note of a flute. She knew she loved him entirely, and she knew he loved her. There were three parts to him, and two of those loved her and the third counted not at all. In the loud clamour of the war he was waging, his hand would go out for her, and she would be at his side, like a flame. And in the dusk of the evening she would be there, too, like some soul released at twilight to wander sweetly-scented under the friendly silence of the moon. In the clang and clamour of his plans, the high notes of life, she had been adding enthusiasm to his enthusiasm, fire to his fire until the will of them melted and blended like some wind-driven flame.

"He needed me then, and I was there, and again I will be there, when he needs me."

And there had been the other times, too, apart from these high notes, when she had felt her heart so close to his, and his to hers, that they seemed but one great common artery. At times, in the dusk of evening, with the great honey-coloured moon coming out of the East, and the little sounds of night-time in the air; or on afternoons along the calm New England shore, when all seemed asleep except for the murmur of the waves on the little stones, and the nodding of wind-bent flowers—at times like these, a score of occasions, had they felt utterly one, and his arms had gone out to her and his eager mouth, and his lips had on them words of love and great dreams for the future.

"No!" she had said. "No! No!" And her heart had uttered: "Not yet!"

For she knew in her inmost spirit, recognizing

by some sort of intuition, that all the repressed eagerness of his young years must now be blown off, like some excess of steam. He wanted a time for himself, and that he should have. Later on he would be satisfied to labour in his own particular line, and achieve greatness in it. She did not want to kill that high, merry spirit in him. No! She wanted that to live, being part of him; but at present, in its wild rushing state it would not be understood by the grey-headed wiseacres of his surroundings. But she had not dreamed that already he would have a quasi-national reputation as a merry-Andrew, be alluded to as New York's favourite buffoon. John Mongel! who had done so much! in whom there was so much!

"I will go to New York," she decided. There was no thought in her mind that she would not succeed. She was a tower of strength unto him, a mighty bulwark, and nothing should prevail against her.

V

I wonder why they called her Sappho Buchanan, that small, golden-brown woman, with the full, laughing face and the brown eyes; a mole beneath

THE EVIL MEN DO

her right eye and a mole on her chin, full of curves, laughing-eyed, bronze-haired?

You might easily misunderstand Sappho. The old New Yorkers shun her as much as they can; they say she is unconventional. The staid New Englanders like her not at all; they dub her that careful, terrible word "fast." A few men like her; they are those who can see behind that harshness in her eyes, that flippant, hard speech; that eternal craving for amusement. There must have been a man, sometime, somewhere, who treated her harshly. I can see that in certain moments—at the playing of certain songs. The harshness, the flippancy will drop from her face for an instant like some Greek mummer's mask. Only an instant, though, does that long-range melting look last. It is succeeded by a laugh as harsh as that of a very bad actor playing a villain's part.

Since she had come out of the west, four years ago, daughter of old Buchanan, the peach king—he who had gambled and roystered and drunk until he dropped in his tracks, the death he wished for—sponsored by a few kind friends and many kindly millions, there had been a half-dozen men who had proposed to marry her. Tod Randolph, who swore there was never a horse or woman he could not tame. Then he met his Waterloo. There was De Peyster Keogh, that queer mixture of Dutch and Connaught Irish, urbane, witty, very vogue as he termed himself, most abominably poor. His ears must have tingled as she told him what she thought of fortune hunters. There was also Philippe de Cohen, self-styled artist, some occupational parasite, interior decorator or what-not, a creature of candles and shaded rooms. He made rather a notable speech about passion, and got the marks of five feminine muscular fingers across his cheek. . . .

"To the devil with her!" old Tod Randolph swore most unchivalrously. He was hard hit, the old sportsman! "What she wants is an angel from heaven who can ride amateur steeplechase, play par golf, and drink fifty cocktails and not show it. And begad! she won't get it," he concluded most reasonably.

And so she went down in the minds of all as one of those occasional woman-types averse to matrimony. Actually they knew her to be a good pal, as the word is, to be a good sportsman, good for a dance, good for a hunt, good for a flirtation—to a certain point, but no further.

"I don't think there's the man born she could care for," they used to shake their heads.

THE EVIL MEN DO

Came down to New York John L'hommedieu Mongel, curly-haired, jaunty, handsome, claiming the welcome that was his in fee simple by virtue of his smile. He walked into the city with an air of "Here we are at last! I'm sorry I'm late, but let's begin with the programme." None could resist him, no more than they could resist a smiling, unknown child toddling into a room-full of grown-ups.

The disillusionment that we spoke of before, that cad's conduct of some man, had made Sappho Buchanan's eyes wary. She trusted none. There were some she could tolerate, and a few she liked, but over none could she become enthusiastic. Before this vague, unmentionable drama had occurred, in her own state of California—the one subject over which she was not cynical—she had been very happy, very joyous, singing just as birds sing, and taking as little thought of the morrow as did the clover blossoms in the grass. There still remained in her a fount of gaiety, but restrained, sophisticated, harshly wordly-wise. But when John Mongel came into her vision she could have clapped her hands in applause.

"There am I!" she shouted within her. "The real I!"

His smile captured her; his radiance; his air

THE EVIL MEN DO

of being on a holiday. All the genial springtime of old seemed to wake within her, after the four lurid, lonely winters her heart had known. Spring broke for her into a rustling green, and a murmuring of crickets, high, pure moons and the swish of the south wind. She was like a child again, happy, playful, innocuously theatrical. Poor little pagan lady!

And as surely as two magnetized pieces of steel will attract each other, so were attracted John Mongel and Sappho Buchanan. Until his arrival she had been the wag, the wit, the scapegrace of her world, but when he came she was content and glad to be his second and assistant. There were things she suggested, like his famous bet that he would get breakfast, dinner, and supper from three different people in a single day, without asking them for it and without paying either. She liked to see one man who could enter heartily into the spirit of things, play the game as a sportsman. There was never a moment when he palled on her.

Little by little she began to figure to herself what life might be with him—a succession of hedonistic days in a mature child's paradise where the sun would be always shining and a new game for each hour. Occasionally, too, there would be sweet, vague twilight stirrings and a tender sort of love-making. He had never spoken a word of that to her except in jest, as on that day at Greenwich.

"What will you give me?" she asked, looking down the first hole with her trained athlete's eye.

"My life; my wealth; my soul!" he told her huskily. And then with a laugh: "I'll give you nothing, you crook! You play a Metropolitan seven."

And now for the first time since she came east her eyes lost their hardness and became dancing again, dancing with natural happiness, not the sophisticated measure of her cynical life. Her laugh lost its harshness and bubbled spontaneously from her heart. New York, lynx-eyed for scandal or for romance, noticed it immediately.

"Damned if that Buchanan girl hasn't fallen in love!" exploded old Brigadier-General Baines to his cowed wife. "With that Mongel puppy, too. I thought she had sense."

Very indefinite it was to Sappho Buchanan, a honey-coloured dream, an aromatic possibility. Until now it had sufficed her to be by his side, smiling with him, enjoying their merry triumph, hardly thinking that there ever could come a time when they should go their separate ways. He not to be there, and she not to be there, and they not

THE EVIL MEN DO

laughing—that seemed incredible. And then the diaphanous possibility, becoming each day more amorphous, that they should enter, with minister and acolyte, with candle and book and bell, into that closest of intimacies under heaven. So it seemed, until one day the fear of separation came up, and she knew she wanted him and wanted him badly. She met Eleanor Godley.

It was at a dinner on Madison Avenue, a vague, dreary affair with Metropolitan singers warbling disgustedly in the background somewhere, and a dreary dance to follow. To Sappho Buchanan came Mongel, by his side a tall young woman who moved like a queen, slender, straight, with her face proud like a challenge and somehow very gentle. But for her chiselled Grecian features she might have been an Egyptian daughter of a King, so black her hair was, and so steady and frank and brave her eyes. And by her side Mongel walked, proudly, too.

"Eleanor," he said enthusiastically, "this is Miss Buchanan, about whom I was talking to you, the girl who played polo at Palm Beach. The best in the world!"

Sappho had heard him speak of an Eleanor Godley, describing her vaguely, as a man will, but she had never imagined her such as she saw before her now.

She watched her for an instant, standing by Mongel as though it were her rightful place. She watched Mongel's admiration of her, his happiness at being by her side. There was a momentary look of consternation in her eyes; and then a veiled hard look that crept through the conventional smile—the look of battle.

"I want you two girls to be friends," Mongel went on enthusiastically.

"I should like to," Eleanor Godley said gently. "I should like to very much." In an instant, with that intuitive gift of hers, that rapid, infallible probing, she had understood Sappho Buchanan before her, had sensed somewhere in the back years the wealing cut of a spiritual lash; the hard laughing battle against barren life; the hope that was in the girl. She was very sorry for Sappho Buchanan, heartily sorry.

VI

For weeks now she had been worried. In Fall River, disaffection among labour had been brewing until it burst in open unrest through the streets. From the papers, from her cousins the Richardsons, Eleanor had heard of it until it became the one

THE EVIL MEN DO

big thing in her mind. She spoke of it continually to Mongel, at lunch in the Ritz, riding in the Park, strolling up Fifth Avenue in the afternoon.

"I'm sure you could do something, John," she pleaded. "Nobody has the influence you have."

"Eleanor girl," he told her gravely, "I went up twice. I'm not very popular with the other employers on account of the system in my place. And I've got no right to harangue other men's employees. There is no trouble in my own mills. I'd do everything I could, but I can't do anything."

"I understand," she said. "The men will tell you you've got no right to counsel them to go back to conditions you wouldn't stand yourself in your own place. And the other owners would say you were sowing disaffection for your own ends."

From her uncle Leonard—him of the Commerce Commission—she learned that Will Johnson was in town, Will Johnson, the labour agitator. The Stormy Petrel, he was called. That was serious news.

"The employers must give way, or the men. There'll be a strike otherwise, and then——"

"And then?" she asked him.

"And then I'll be able to do something," he said. His jaw set. "And I'll do it."

THE EVIL MEN DO

And do it he would, that she knew, and she thrilled as to the thought of bugles and drums. She wanted him to justify himself, to give egress to the greatness within him. She wanted him for herself; that she was beginning to understand better every day. And into his voice, too, there was creeping an undercurrent of tenderness toward her, never evident in his dealings with other women.

She had met Sappho Buchanan many and many times since, and always in that dashing eye she had read battle. For Sappho wanted him sincerely, poor girl! she knew, but she should not have him. For Sappho wanted him for himself and for herself, but she, Eleanor, wanted him to have his career also. The lips of Sappho Buchanan might drip as the honeycomb, and even though she, Eleanor, was beautiful as Tirzah, comely as Jerusalem, yet should her husband be known in the gates, when he sat among the elders of the land.

VII

She had just dropped the receiver of the telephone. "I've been trying to get Mongel everywhere," her uncle Leonard had telephoned from New Bedford. "They all went out on a strike this morning, except Mongel's people. Presented a sudden ultimatum at noon and walked out a half hour ago. Johnson's preaching hell loose . . . Mongel might talk to them now. . . . He's the only man could handle them. . . . Get him, for God's sake, Eleanor. . . ."

"I'll get him, Uncle Leonard," she answered succinctly.

He evidently wasn't at home, then, for it was there that Leonard had telephoned. Should she begin a round of his clubs, telephoning each one? No! His man Nocka would know, but he would not tell a chance caller on the phone. She whipped from Washington Square North to Forty-fifth Street overriding traffic like a juggernaut. The Japanese valet received her with a courteous intake of breath.

"Nocka," she told him frankly, "It's a matter of life or death for me to see Mr. Mongel. There's trouble at New Bedford. Pack Mr. Mongel's bag immediately. See about trains in an hour. Where is he now?"

The Japanese looked at her a long moment.

"He's having tea at Miss Buchanan's, Miss Godley," he told her.

She swept up Madison Avenue to Eighty-fifth Street.

THE EVIL MEN DO

The elevator boy did not wait to announce her. She was not the sort that is kept waiting. She turned toward the Buchanan apartment. The maid opened the door.

"You needn't announce me," Eleanor said.

So hurried was she that she forgot her way and blundered into the dining-room. She heard voices, the voices of Mongel and Sappho Buchanan, laughing. Then an instant of silence. Then startling clear, startling tense, the voice of Sappho:

"John, old boy, why don't you marry me?"

A moment of silence, then Mongel laughed heartily.

"Why, of course, Sappho. What day would you like?"

Where was that door? This was no time for fooling. Again came Sappho's voice, strangely nervous.

"I'm not joking, John. Why don't you?"

Eleanor stopped suddenly. The blood left her face in one swirling ebb. She could hear Mongel's embarrassed stutter.

"I don't quite understand."

"I don't know what you'll think of me," went on Sappho's tones, more strained than ever. "It sounds so terribly immodest. But it just struck

THE EVIL MEN DO

me, do you see? We like each other so much—so much to be in each other's company—I sort of wondered—why it couldn't go on——"

For a moment Eleanor Godley was terrified. She could not break in on that. She was afraid to go out as she came. She might be noticed, and they would know she had heard part of it. That would be terrible.

"I'm a brazen hussy, I know, but I'm in love with you, John Mongel."

So, unwillingly, she was to be a witness of this awful thing. A great sense of vicarious shame swept over Eleanor Godley, flooding her crimson. It was as though some other woman had bared herself in a room full of men. She put her fingers to her ears, but dropped them again. The strain of her own fate was too much. She could imagine that big, spacious sitting-room. Sappho standing, perhaps, leaning her back against the sombre Norman vestiary, her glorious bronze head lowered in embarrassment, her fingers playing nervously at the girdle of her frock; Mongel sitting very still, his head averted, his hands clasped.

"I've been in love only once before, John, and I thought it was the one and only time I should ever be. The man was a rotter, and I've been brooding over it like a schoolgirl ever since, and it was nothing—a few talks in a moonlit garden and some harmless kisses, but this is real, John. So real it makes me do this. Good Lord!" she laughed nervously, "I believe I'm crying."

"Please, Sappho, for Heaven's sake——"

"I've been very unhappy," she went on. "You know—about my father . . . and about that other thing I told you of. And when you came I was happy again. I remember singing one night, after that day at Greenwich . . . the first time I'd sung from my heart for years. And I've been thinking how happy we could be all our years together. We'd go everywhere. You've never been abroad and I want to go with you there . . . to be with you in Paris in the spring, and to show you the Côte d'Azur, so blue you would not believe it, John. And to go with you to Epsom, to the Derby, in a drag, John . . . to be with you everywhere, every day, every hour. . . ."

"Sappho girl, listen to me——"

"And it isn't as if I were only a good pal, John, but you could love me. Only one man has kissed me, and those were the harmless girlish kisses, not the kisses of a woman." Her voice grew stifled as though it were coming through her hands. "And my hair comes down to my knees, John, like a cloak . . . and my feet are as small and as white as any woman's . . . and I am queer little dimples all over. . . ."

"For God's sake, Sappho!" Mongel had jumped to his feet with a clatter.

"We are both rich, you and I, John, and we can do what we please. And if you had no money, John, you could have all mine, every cent, even to the little trinkets on my hands. And if I had none, I would go out and beg on the streets so that you would not want. . . ."

Through the passageway Eleanor was stumbling blindly out, her eyes closed as though trying to keep back the tears in them. Suddenly somewhere in the apartment a telephone rang imperatively, rang once, rang twice, as though in harsh command. She remembered the telephone from New Bedford. Her back straightened. She swung about. A few steps and she was in the room. Mongel, embarrassed, on the point of tears himself, was standing by the vestiary. Opposite him was Sappho Buchanan, blindly weeping. Eleanor Godley stepped up to him.

"John," she said, "they've gone out on strike. Uncle Leonard telephoned you must come at once."

"When?"

"An hour ago."

"I must hurry."

"I told Nocka to pack for you and look up trains. I'm coming, too."

"You can't," he told her. "It's going to be no place for a woman."

"John," she looked at him squarely, "It's the place for me!"

He turned around to the Buchanan girl.

"Sappho," he said very tenderly, "I'm sorry. I've got to go."

Her face was streaming with tears, but she threw her head up proudly and looked at him.

"Good-bye, John, old boy," she put her hand out impulsively and caught his in a quick grip. "Good-bye, and let's forget it."

He stood for an instant, uncertain. Eleanor looked at him.

"Go on. I'll be after you in a minute."

She went straight up to Sappho and put her hands on her shoulders.

"I'm sorry, my dear," she whispered. "I'm sorry from the bottom of my heart."

The bronze head dropped heavily. Then the brown eyes looked upward.

THE EVIL MEN DO

"You'll be good to him, won't you?" she whispered.

"For your sake, too, my dear," said Eleanor Godley, and she walked down the passage to where Mongel was pounding impatiently at the elevator bell.

VIII

About the platform in the middle of the square the dark sea of bodies waved intermittently, as the orator with the hatchet-face and the grey-hair swung forward and backward in passionate gestures. The white teeth of the man would snap after a sentence with the suggestive snap of a wolf. Occasionally there would be the rapid put-put of conversation; the clapping of hands like the cracking of sticks; the roar of applause like the swelling note of an organ.

"The flax in the field is tended. The trees for their mills are fed in good soil. The silkworm is given the best of mulberry leaves. But what is the wage the worker earns? A bed a convict would not have; food at which the employer's Airedale would turn up his nose; clothes the employer's servants would despise; and vermin!"

THE EVIL MEN DO

The roar of the square's applause had changed from admiration of the speaker's period to a savage, sinister resonance that resembled the angry humming of wasps. The Stormy Petrel smiled. He was getting under their skins, as his saying was.

"And these out-and-out oppressors, these feudal barons of labour, are not the worst. They know only one way of oppression. But there are others. The cat-a-mountain is not as dangerous as the copperhead. The diving gannet catches less fish than the angler with his scientific rod. There are those of you who were told frankly you could go to hell. But there are others fooled and cajoled, by honeyed words and cunning seeming reforms." He took a step forward and raised his fist and voice. "Whose men refused to come in this demonstration for the workers' rights? Whose men are not in this great assembly? John Mongel's! But out, by God! they'll come, if we must tear the mills about their ears."

There was an instant's silence at that, a hurried murmur, an altercation, as though some were for it, some against.

"Look you!" Johnson hurried on passionately. "Mongel's men are at their work, hurrying to and from. They sort his silk, they dry and throw it.

THE EVIL MEN DO

The men stand at the looms, sweating at the labour of dogs. But where is Mongel? You don't know? Well, I'll tell you. He is down in New York, dancing, gambling, drinking, spending his money with fast women——"

There was a movement through the crowd as of a driving wedge, a set of burly men in tweeds, a well-set up figure among them, and the suspicion of a woman in white. They fought their way to the edge of the platform.

"Where is Mongel? I will tell you about him." Johnson pulled a paper from his pocket. "Where is Mongel? 'At Mrs. da Costa's garden party among the expected guests for Thursday's function are John L'hommedieu Mongel——' There's where he is, at a garden party, dressed prettily, drinking tea and eating cakes and talking nonsense to society women while his workers grind out their lives for him. There's where Mongel is——"

"You lie, Johnson," there came snapping from the base of the platform. "John Mongel is here."

He turned to Eleanor Godley.

"You stay here," he told her. "MacKenzie, you and Willis and Hoagland keep around her."

"I'm coming up," she said decisively.

"You are not," he snapped.

THE EVIL MEN DO

"Please, John," she pleaded. "Please. I want to be with you no matter what comes."

"She'll be all right, Mister John," MacKenzie told him. "Most of them know her. She'll come to no harm."

He clambered up on the platform and held his hand out to her. There was a faint cheering and then a storm of hisses.

"So you're here, Mr. Mongel?" the Stormy Petrel declaimed sneeringly. "We called for you and you came. Now that you're here, what are you going to say?"

Mongel walked forward to him, and looked him for an instant in the face. His left arm shot out like a piston, his right hooked heavily over. Johnson dropped with a crash. The agitator struggled to his feet, and went down again before a stinging uppercut. He lay unconscious in a grotesque heap.

For a moment the crowd had been thunderstruck, dazed into inaction, open-mouthed as spectators at some super-dramatic play. Mongel walked to the edge of the platform, taking off his gloves.

"That is what the first sensible man among you should have done."

His eye roamed over the crowd, glinting dangerously.

THE EVIL MEN DO

"So in another minute you would have gone down to John Mongel's mills, smashing them because his operatives are happy and contented, so to-night you would have had the militia firing into you at your barricades; in a week you would be starving, and the police would be clubbing you as your pickets slugged the blacklegs on their way to work! What sort of madmen are you?"

He turned to the committee of strikers on the platform and pointed to the prostrate Johnson.

"Take that man away!" he ordered. Two or three of them jumped forward to help him off the platform.

"Now listen to me, you people, gathered here by a knave for a foolish end—listen to me! My workmen are not flies caught by honey; they are honest people doing honest work and getting an honest wage from an honest employer. They are my men. They trust me. I trust them. And if you were my men you would get the same thing and you would not be out here to-day——"

"But we're not!" a wild-eyed fanatic in the crowd screamed. "We'll get these things yet from our employers——"

"You'll get what you're worth, my lad, and not a cent more." He turned to the crowd. "A strike

THE EVIL MEN DO

is always a waste," he said, "an intense waste to you, an ultimate waste to your employer. But a waste it is in every way, and of industry, earth's biggest commodity. Frankly and straightly I will say this: Some of your demands are justified, and not all."

A rabid line about the platform began a rumble of protest. Mongel held up his hand.

"You have got no right to the capital of the works—no more than the workman without tools has to the tools of another man. But you have a right to a fair, comfortable wage, according to your station in the scale of skill. At all events you have a right to a decent livelihood. There ends labour. The business end of things is not your province—not the profits; and the loss; not anything. A fair wage for fair work—that is yours."

He raised himself to his full height and put out his hand.

"Go down to my factories and ask any of my operatives if I am a fair man. Ask them if I keep my promises. From the office boy to the manager they will tell you that I do.

"Go back to your work now and I will see your employers, and I will fight for you as I would fight for myself. Go back and I will get you from your employers what rights are coming to you, not a tittle less, not a hundredth more. Go back to your work. I will handle them as I am handling you this noon. Go back to your work."

The mob was chattering excitedly, like innumerable birds. Once more Mongel raised his hand.

"And if I cannot show them what is right and just, I will get enough capital in the East, by God! to hire you all at a fair basis, and I will break these men like a rotten twig."

He watched them dispersing, like some black cloud, breaking up, disappearing. As he stood up straight on the platform, like some reviewing general, he felt a hand clasp his. Eleanor was looking at him with her eyes aflame.

"I knew you could do it, John," she was whispering throatily. "I knew you could. There was none but you could do it. Not one!"

IX

They were running north from Aiken and, staying overnight in New York, they had gone, so as to avoid the Ritz and the old places where his name was as the name of one dead—to a Broadway res-

THE EVIL MEN DO

taurant for dinner. On Eleanor's slim hand as yet the gold circlet was strange-feeling, unaccustomed. Her fine Greek face seemed to radiate beauty, her great eyes to sparkle like deep, precious stones. Her husband was leaning toward her.

"Are you sure now," he was bantering, "you would not rather have gone to Europe than have returned to the grimy north?"

"I want to see you up there, John," she told him throbbingly. "I want to see your work sweep over the place like May west wind, clean and big and earth-ripening——"

A singer, an obese, dark man, had come on the cabaret platform at the end of the dining-room. A few notes from an accompanist and the plaintive minors of *Lyrics from a Persian Garden* filled the room:

> "*Some for the glories of this world,*"
>   he sang, "*and some
> Sigh for the Prophet's Paradise to come.
> Ah, take the cash, and let the credit go,
> Nor heed the rumble of a distant drum.*"

"Do you hear the drums, John?" she said. She gripped his hand and threw back her head exultantly. "Do you hear the drums? And in a little time your armies will be marching on the road!"

VIII

AS TO IMPEDIMENTS

At times he felt sure she knew, and for a moment his heart would pause in its natural function, as a surprised frightened man will stumble, stop, go on, in his gait.

And then he would say to himself; no! It's impossible. How could she know?

But her eyes troubled him, her great luminous grey eyes. There was a puzzled, watching quality in them that disturbed him. He had seen them under other emotions—moist with tenderness, gentle and hushed with dreaming, cloudy with passion, bright and beaming with certain joy, but never had he seen that watching quality in them, that made him feel like a stranger. Good God! Could she know? And how could she know? Perhaps, a tremor seized him, he had let fall a word in his sleep, a phrase, a something or other, and she had pieced it together and circumstanced the truth from it. Perhaps that was it. But he didn't talk in his sleep. Could he be certain of that? He had set a guard on his lips all day but his

AS TO IMPEDIMENTS

heart, his mind, was full to bursting. And was it not possible that his lips would utter his thoughts when his normal mind was asleep and the mysterious subconscious self free while his human frame slumbered? It might. You never could tell. But could Anne have reconstructed anything from the few phrases he might have mumbled? No! no, no!

Could Pilar have written? Could Pilar be in New York? No! She thought he was in England. Pilar knew no English. It was a million to one chance of her ever hearing, and even if she did, she wouldn't know what to do.

And yet Anne, he felt, knew something, suspected something.

The thing was preying on his mind—that was it. Silly! Occasionally he remembered the words of the clergyman at their wedding:

"I require and charge ye both, as ye will answer at the dreadful day of judgment when the secrets of all hearts shall be disclosed, that if either of you know any impediment why ye may not be lawfully joined together in matrimony, ye do now confess it. For be ye well assured that if any persons are joined together otherwise than as God's word doth allow, their marriage is not lawful."

The minatory formula had called up in him a sense

AS TO IMPEDIMENTS

of fear on the morning the minister had pronounced it. "Lawful!" Of course the marriage wasn't legal, but after all was he to be tied all his life to that Spanish woman in Colombia, doomed for ever to a wife unworthy of him, just because of the lure of the tropics, of a romance of an old patio, of a moon treacherously sentimental . . . ? But could anything be more lawful than a good man wedding with a fine woman? Wasn't it eminently suitable, this marriage. Legality be damned! This was humanly lawful.

But again it occurred to him; didn't this mean against God's law?

And then he laughed; after all, this was the twentieth century. God! Tut! tut! For priests and women, maybe, but for men, no!

And yet the formula rang in his ears with a sinister reverberation, giving him the same sense of immediate, inevitable danger, as though from the bridge of his own ship, in an unknown channel in a foggy sea the bell buoy of some murderous rock, tolling, tolling, tolling. . . .

"Oh, I say, Anne," he asked his wife in his beautifully modulated voice, "tell me, did you ever know of me to talk in my sleep?"

She was bending over some sewing so he could not see her face.

AS TO IMPEDIMENTS

"Why, sometimes," she answered evenly. "You mumble things. A sentence, a name. Oh, yes, you talk in your sleep. Quite often. I suppose everyone does."

"What? Not really!" But his heart belied the cheery flippancy of his tone.

II

When he had married Pilar, three years before, he was master of a passenger line that went from New York to Jamaica, thence to Colón in Panama, thence to the Colombian posts, Cartagena, Puerto Colombia, Santa Marta. But within the year of his marriage he acquired a new berth aboard a ten-thousand tonner running from New York to the Leewards and Virginia, and thence to British Guiana and back again to New York. Pilar he left in her own house in Cartagena, the cool white house with its flower-filled patio, beneath the wall the King of Spain built many centuries agone.

Six months away from Pilar and he had begun to despise her. She was all right, you know, when a man feels that way. But damn it all! she was hardly the wife for an officer and a gentleman—he was in the

AS TO IMPEDIMENTS

Royal Naval Reserve. Yes, she was young and beautiful, I grant you. A lady, as ladies went in Colombia. She had a little money of her own; her own house. But she wasn't a gentlewoman, as the English word is. She wasn't the sort of wife you'd care to bring home and exhibit to your people. He was jolly glad his friends, his brother officers, didn't know he had married her. They thought—they understood it was just one of those affairs. . . . It was better so.

And then on a trip he had met Anne Farum, admired her, saw the lasting qualities of her slim Norse beauty, fell in love with her.

She had come with an invalid mother for a convalescing voyage, and for all of five weeks they were together. He had every opportunity of admiring her. What appealed to him most was the tremendous difference between her and Pilar. She was tall and slight. Pilar was little and round as a kitten. Her hair was flaxen and her eyes grey while Pilar's hair was black and her eyes black, too. Her voice was crisp and ringing, Pilar's was low and throaty—a voluptuous contralto. There was a great reserve about Anne Farum. About Pilar there was none—she gave herself freely as the wind. Anne was ever active. All Pilar did was to rest and dream—dream of him. Anne

AS TO IMPEDIMENTS

was more of his own age, she was twenty-six and he was thirty, and Pilar was only seventeen.

On the whole she was a wife to be proud of. Pilar, he felt, was an acknowledgment of weakness. To marry a Spanish woman of Cartagena, though she were of the proudest blood of Spain married to Inca ladies, was something like going native in India. It simply wasn't done.

He thought the matter over quickly. Pilar was a foreigner. It didn't much matter about her, she would forget him and marry one of her own kind. Perhaps not marry, for she was under the domination of her creed which did not permit divorce. But she would find a man, more fitted to her.

So quietly he set about marrying Anne Farum.

A ship's captain of latter days has one of the most peculiar positions in the world. To him has descended the royalty of the master of clipper days—the men who fought men and tempests, and dragged their cloud of sail through the teeth of hell to Java Head or Frisco Bay; racing against competitors who sailed their argosies of commerce as though they were cup challengers; buying with the shrewdness of merchants; docking and warping out their great dolphins as though they were catboats. To-day the ship's captain has nothing but position and deference. The

AS TO IMPEDIMENTS

skilled engineers below sail his boat. National legislations have made his craft safe as a trolley car. He has less risk on his ocean voyage than a truck-driver has on the Boston Post Road. He has the pay of a milkman, the social graces of a grocer, the mental equipment of a bank clerk, the work of a draughtman's helper. And yet he is deferred to, to some extent reverenced. The tinge of the aureola of Vasco da Gama, and Amerigo Vespucci, and Columbus the Genoese hang about him still. *Stat magni nominis umbra!* There remains the shadow of a great name.

And Richard Wyndham, "master mariner," was the one to make the most of it. Tall, thin, slick and black-haired, with melancholy, inconstant eyes, with regular features, with his eternal talk that he wasn't really a merchant skipper but a navy man, with graces he had picked up here and there—now from an actor, here from a planter, there from a consul. He could make himself very engaging to any woman. He looked tremendously romantic in his white ducks, as he went on his morning round of inspection or stood on the bridge, talking to the officer of the watch.

He made everything tremendously comfortable for Anne Farum. Stewards rushed like terriers at her slightest wish. The bridge was free to her when she wished. He was always by her side in port or entering

AS TO IMPEDIMENTS

a harbour. She began to grow fond of him—he was such a nice fellow.

And then a great respect grew up in her for him. All the ship's crew were deferential. And she made the pardonable mistake of thinking the respect was for him personally, and not for his office. He looked so commanding. To think that this immensity of steel was his to be responsible for and to do as he wished with. She loved to hear him command as they made a landfall.

"A little more to starboard."

And the quartermaster in the wheelhouse behind would repeat the command.

"A little more to starboard, sir."

"Starboard a little faster. Hard—o'—starboard!"

"Hard o' starboard, sir!"

As they made port he leaned over the bridge, oblivious and contemptuous of the meek pilot on whose shoulders the whole responsibility rested. Anne loved to watch him like that, leaning on the bridge-rail, bronzed, aloof, as the liner surged gently through the indigo bay.

And so for a month with romance in the air like a perfume, they wandered through the murmuring Carib seas, past Dutch and Danish ports, French and English. Up from Africa the trade winds came,

AS TO IMPEDIMENTS

a gentle, eternal pushing. And the little trade cumulus of cloud in the sky made the sky only bluer and farther away. . . .

It was on this homeward voyage he decided to speak. The Southern Cross had slipped beneath the sky—the true cross; only the false was visible. A whispering night, with a thin new moon over the Bahamas, like a golden horn.

"Miss Farum—Anne—it seems so cruel for us who have been together so much, never to meet again. When you go out of my life, my life will be appallingly empty. Anne, dear Anne, could you not stay and make it full?"

"What—what do you mean, Captain Wyndham?" Her voice was trembling, and her heart, too.

"Would you not—marry me?" The words came from his lips with a tearing feeling within him. "And let us be together all our lives, as we were this month."

"I cared for someone once," her voice came low and pained from the shadows. "We quarrelled. He went away. He went out of my life entirely. But I don't think I can ever quite get him out of my heart or mind. You wouldn't want me—so—Richard?"

"I would want you any way, any way, dearest one."

AS TO IMPEDIMENTS

She said nothing.

"Couldn't you care for me? You care for me a little already, don't you, Anne?"

"I think I do, Richard."

III

Now they were married and settled in their house, and all going well for them. He had received the billet of port captain in New York and he often thought to himself, it was just as well he had. For Randolph Scofield, her first love, turned up after they had been married a month. A stocky, muscular man, with eyes very blue, very hard, he seemed tremendously frank. He introduced himself and congratulated them. Anne never blinked.

"Back again, Randolph."

"Back again, Anne."

A strained, unpleasant evening talking of South Africa, whence Scofield had just come. At ten he rose to go.

"Good-bye, Anne."

"Good-bye, Randolph."

Wyndham insisted on seeing him to the elevator.

AS TO IMPEDIMENTS

"Do drop in and see us again," he said. "Always pleased, y'know, to see Anne's old friends."

Scofield squared his jaws and shoulders. Looked the husband in the eye.

"Captain Wyndham," he said, "four years ago I was dreadfully in love with Anne. We quarrelled because I wanted her to marry me when I hadn't a job, hadn't a penny. I said nothing to her but I went out to make money so that I could marry her. I came back with it. I found she was married. I thought after all that if I saw her I would get over the disappointment. I find the same old Anne and myself as much in love with her as ever. So I shan't come back, sir. Thank you for your invitation."

"Oh, yes! of course! Naturally! Wise thing——"

The elevator stopped at the floor with a clang. Scofield grasped the sailor's hand.

"Well, good luck! Let me tell you, Captain Wyndham, you're a lucky man."

Lucky! Damn his bloody impertinence! He was the better man, that was all.

IV

Of Randolph Scofield Anne never made mention. There was no change in her attitude towards her

AS TO IMPEDIMENTS

husband. She only spoke a little less. Her eyes grew deeper, and he was more in love with her than ever.

But night and day the fear haunted him that she would discover his first marriage, that she knew of it now. Yes, she knew of it now. She must know of it, else what meant the puzzled look in her grey eyes?

And then one night he could no longer stand it. Shrewdly he figured out what he would do. She loved him, he flattered himself, loved him better far than her first love. And when a woman loved, he had somewhere read, there is nothing she will not forgive. And after all, what was there to forgive, but that he had loved her so well, he had committed a crime? Surely she would love him the more for that! The best he could do then was to confess outright, to throw himself on her mercy. And when a man was at her mercy a woman was most tender. What did the French say: *tout savoir c'est tout pardonner* ? To know all is to forgive all. And moreover, since he feared she knew it, it would be just as well.

She was sitting in the bow-window of her apartment overlooking Central Park, when he entered that Autumn afternoon. Grey-eyed, in a grey dress, in a warm grey room, all composed into a picture Whistler might have painted, a symphony of quiet, delicate strength.

AS TO IMPEDIMENTS

.nne," he stepped into the room and closed the door. There was a theatrical quality to his accent, movement, posture, "there is something on my mind —worries me—I must tell you."

"Yes, Richard." Crisp but low came her tones from the window.

"Before I met you—two years before—in Cartagena—I met a girl. A Spanish girl. And— and—I sort of lost my head. Loneliness, you know— the tropics—perhaps a touch of sun. I married her. I married her—I married her—and my God! she is still alive!"

She turned to him with a deep inbreathing of dismay.

"You married her and she is still alive."

"Yes, you knew, didn't you? Didn't you know?"

"Know? How could I?"

"I thought—I thought——" his voice wavered and died.

"Oh, but Richard! This is some monstrous joke. You are ill. You are imagining things."

"I would to God I were!"

She rose and walked toward him steadily. He flinched as she came. She was silent a moment.

"Do you mean that you dared to marry me while you had a wife still living—a legal wife?"

AS TO IMPEDIMENTS

"I dared anything for you, Anne."

"Faugh!"

Her brows knitted together as though she could not fix her mind on the problem. She spoke again in a puzzled way.

"You mean I am not married to you at all."

"In the eyes of God——"

"Keep God's name out of your mouth, you fool. I am not your wife—legally."

"No, but Anne——"

"You have no hold on me at all?"

"None but what my love gives me. Anne! Anne! Can't you see? I loved you so much I dared."

She looked at him calmly for an instant, very detached as though she had never seen him before. All she spoke was two words:

"Shut up!"

The crisp, cold vernacular acted on him like a dash of icy water in the face, making him understand where he was, what he had done, what he was saying. All elements of great drama crumpled. This was the woman who he thought would have come to him with humid eyes and outstretched arms and said, "Love, what does it matter? The past is gone. You dared and did for my sake. You loved me. That is enough. Let us never speak a word of it

AS TO IMPEDIMENTS

again. Don't speak. Just kiss." There she was, self-possessed and frigid before him, and from her lips came a crisp, contemptuous command, such as might have been addressed to a barking, troublesome dog.

"Oh, shut up!"

There was another interval of silence. She was thinking. When she spoke it was as to an inimical, contemptible stranger.

"You'd better go back to your wife in Cartagena."

"But, Anne——"

"Go back to your wife."

"Anne, this is ridiculous. We must act sensibly."

She was going over to the telephone on the sitting-room table. She turned and looked at him.

"You had better go away," she informed him. "I am going to call up Randolph Scofield, and if you are here when he comes, or are anywhere he can find you, he is going to kill you. So you'd better go away and hide."

"Anne, you really mustn't——"

But she gave an amused, hard, bitter laugh.

"Yes, he will kill you. I can promise you that!"

And suddenly Wyndham slunk out of the door, like a whipped dog. For an instant he stood in the street, in dull amaze. And then sharp panic touched

AS TO IMPEDIMENTS

him, and he began running, running, running away. . . .

So here again was Cartagena! There the drowsy bay with the leper colony on its spit of sand! There the background of the snow clad mountains! There the torrid town with the wall the King of Spain built—oh, how many centuries ago. There the blue shadows of the public square; the intimate crowding of the churches. There was a place to dream in, the entry to the land of emeralds and parrots and fine gold. But Wyndham was not dreaming.

He had come down a passenger on a fruit boat, and at the office of his own line he had been stopped by the agent and given a letter, the tersest, simplest and most threatening of letters, a letter from Randolph Scofield:

"Anne and I are to be married on the twenty-fourth. If ever you attempt to come into her life again, if ever you are within a reasonable journey of where we are, I will come and kill you."

And Randolph would, he knew. And they were to be married on the twenty-fourth, two days, forty-eight little hours, from to-day.

The agent had looked at him queerly, and hazarded a remark.

AS TO IMPEDIMENTS

"I didn't think you were coming back!"

"And why? Might I ask?"

"Oh, just didn't," the agent was embarrassed.

But when Wyndham came to the house that was Pilar's he found it barricaded, shut, grown about with weeds. And he thought he understood the agent. She had gone away, as he was sure she would have, with another man.

A couple of natives were watching him. Then one shot off down the street suddenly. The other moved away.

"Here, boy. Señora Wyndham? Where is she? Where does she live?"

But the boy just edged away and looked at him with inimical alien eyes.

"Oh, damn!" Wyndham swore. He made his way suddenly toward the centre of the town, and sat at a table on the pavement.

"Bring me a whisky."

He felt growing on him a sensation of having been very badly used. First one woman, for a mistake which any woman who cared for a man would condone and forget, had pitched him out of her life.

"Because," he told himself, "that other chappie had come back from Africa with money. She took advantage of an opening and just put me in the cart. Damn her!"

AS TO IMPEDIMENTS

And not only that, but this native woman must go off with some unwashed "spiggotty." Constancy, it wasn't in them. Damn them all!

"Captain Wyndham?"

Wyndham looked up. A tall, lithe Colombian was smiling at him occultly. He was a young man—years younger than Wyndham. About him was an easy cosmopolitanism. Wyndham discovered suddenly he disliked this young man.

"Oh, yes, I'm Wyndham. What do you want?"

"My name is Rafael de Vengoechen y Hermante," he sat down easily. "I hear you were asking for Señora Wyndham. Señora Wyndham is dead."

"Dead! Dead? And when?"

"Señora Wyndham died on the eighteenth of March of last year."

"Eighteenth of March?" Why, that was two days before he married Anne. "Are you certain of that?"

"Very certain of that, Captain Wyndham, because I was very much in love with your wife, and was looking for you to kill you so I could marry her."

But Wyndham wasn't listening. Good Lord! After all, he was legally married to Anne. Legally married. And she couldn't marry this flame of hers now, on the twenty-fourth, or at any time. Not while he was alive.

AS TO IMPEDIMENTS

"Perhaps you didn't quite understand me. I said: I was looking for you to kill you so that I could marry your wife."

"I don't quite follow."

"Perhaps a little explanation would help." Hermante was still smiling. "You see, Pilar and I were sweethearts in childhood days, and I would have married her, but my people were rich and vain. I was attached to my country's diplomatic service and sent abroad for years. When my father died I came back here to marry Pilar."

"Pilar never mentioned this—ah—attachment to me."

"Very naturally not, Captain Wyndham. Why should she? It was her business and mine, not yours, even though you were married to her. But to continue: When I came back and found her married, and deserted, Captain Wyndham——"

"She was not deserted!"

"I said deserted, Captain Wyndham. When I found that, I decided I would find you and kill you."

"You are a very theatrical young man, and I haven't any time for you. I have to go to the cable office, so you will pardon me——"

He rose, thinking of the cable he would send:

AS TO IMPEDIMENTS

"Pilar died two days before our ceremony. Everything quite legal. Break present plans. Returning immediately." And then he thought he would add these words. "Cannot everything be as it was before, dear heart."

But the Colombian was insistent:

"Please, Captain Wyndham, can't you be patient a moment."

"No, no. I'm going to the cable office."

Even if she didn't have him back, she would never marry Scofield. Not while he was alive.

"You are not going to the cable office, Captain Wyndham."

"And why not, might I ask?"

"Because you are going somewhere else." The Colombian stepped back, and Wyndham looked at him in a puzzled way. He had not had time to be frightened yet. The Colombian took a revolver from his pocket, lifted it, aimed cannily, and shot him neatly through the forehead, as a horse is shot.

Then for the first time the mask of politeness fell from his countenance, and his voice rang out harsh and triumphant:

"Ohé! Scavengers, come quickly. I have shot a dog and it litters up the street!"

IX

HARLEY JOHNSTON, GENTLEMAN

There is an axiom somewhere to the effect that if a man springs of a decent stock, has behind him a decent home, and is fortified by education and culture, he will never deviate from the path of honour and integrity. As the bough is bent, wiseacres say, so will the tree be inclined. Plutarch, most acute of ancient psychologists, remarks on this at length, à propos of the lives of his great men. We believe it, you and I, for it is one of the few rules we go by in estimating values in the game of life.

Another cardinal principle we believe in, you and I, is that once a man has plumbed a certain depth of degradation, there is no hope for him, no toleration, no assistance. The blessed Augustine, kindliest and most human of theologians, tries to grapple with this problem, shakes his head and passes on to the next perplexity. It is a selfish, brazen, inhuman belief, yet we cling to it firmly, you and I. You will remember that every creed, it matters not how cheerfully it preaches the doctrine of repentance and redemption, speaks, too, of "the unforgivable sins."

I am not delivering to you a moral thesis, or descanting on ethical values. I am about to relate a history in which these two cardinal principles are shamefully flouted and set at naught, a history in which a man sinks to a level outside the benevolent sympathy of the priest, or the understanding tolerance of the lowest of crooks, and in which he speeds upward again, as a diver ascends from the depths. For as the black slag which conceals pure metal falls away under the touch of flame, so, by chastening pain and affliction, does a man come back to his estate, and leave behind him the dust and dross of the journey.

In this connection I introduce to you Harley Johnston, gentleman, one time of Magdalen College, Oxford, now dead; Claire Grahame, spinster, of Chester, England, the affianced of Harley Johnston, who mourns for him as a widow for a husband; "Sally" Tolliver, prostitute, of West Thirty-fifth Street, New York, City, now in the Bedford Reformatory. Across the main fabric of my story there runs the faint thread of Ethel Wyckoff, governess, who walked up Fifth Avenue, on a February morning. There are other minor characters, of course, but these are the main persons of my drama. The why and wherefore of the

HARLEY JOHNSTON, GENTLEMAN

play I have mentioned as an announcer moralizes in a Chinese theatre. The action of it I will now unfold. If you are ready, I am. Let us begin.

I

WHEN Harley Johnston came into the world, he arrived at a small manor house and grounds on the Sussex downs that had been depleted, attenuated and shaved by a succession of Johnstons who had held commissions in the army and navy and diplomatic service—services in which one receives the gratitude of one's country and the respect of one's fellowmen, and salaries sufficient to buy cigarettes, to have one's shoes polished, and one's hair cut, but which an economical government never considers in relation to food, housing, or offspring. Wherefore the house of the Sussex Johnstons, having rarely been reinforced through the channels of commerce, successful speculation, or any of the divers ways in which money accrues to people without the direct action of muscular effort, was compelled to look closely and often at a five pound note before releasing it to be used in ways other than were strictly necessary. The slipping of the

HARLEY JOHNSTON, GENTLEMAN

family downward in the financial scale was evidenced by the slipping of the boys downward in the educational scale—one hundred years ago they attended Eton; to-day they skimp to go to a minor public school; of the men in the military scale—four generations before they had graced Guard regiments; now they were satisfied with the unobtrusive "Buffs." The grandsons of tradesmen who served the family a century ago roll past in their limousines, while the old-world ladies of the family drive along in a faded victoria with a faded grey mare and a faded coachman who gardens when he is not driving, and is butler when the needs of the little garden have been attended to.

To this house and this family then, fathered by a stolid but gallant little artillery captain who sleeps —God rest him!—among the gun-limbers of Spion Kop, and mothered by a fair-haired and equally gallant little woman who reads the Bible of mornings and the poems of Elizabeth Barrett Browning in the afternoon, came Harley Johnston, with his destiny prepared for him by tradition and the Johnston code. He would go to the school, go to the college, get his commission in the regiment or join the navy as a spruce middy, or in some corner of England where tradition and the code are understood he would take up the cure of souls, if his call went in that direction, eventually to become pastor there, and bring out an edition of one of the lesser-known Latin or Greek authors, as all old-world pastors do. For him there was to be no marshal's baton, no admiral's cocked hat, nor the apron and gaiters of a bishop. He was born to do the solid and not the brilliant work of his country, as ten generations of Johnstons had done before him, unless——

Unless—and here the old-world ladies and the little fair-haired mother let their imaginations run riot—unless Harley, tenth of the name, married one of those seductive heiresses so common in the Victorian romances they read. Why should he not? they asked. Men did it every day in the week, and there were few men so well fitted to appeal to any woman as the Johnstons—then would be open to him all the avenues of political, naval and military advancement. The glory of the house on the Sussex downs would return to it. The old grey nag would fade into honourable retirement, the dingy drawing-room would be refitted—there would be no more of the shame-faced consultations with the dressmaker over the remodelling of ancient gowns, or the harassing curtailment of hospitality that was forced on them—the scales of the balance would swing them back to the perpendicular for which they were born. God help them, it was very pathetic!

And so Harley grew up from something grotesque and red that refused to go asleep of nights to a slim boy of thirteen in an Eton jacket and a mortarboard cap, and went off to school. And at eighteen he came back; taller, broader, with whitish-fair hair, blue eyes, and the stolid look of the Johnstons, that told you that you might be right but that they weren't sure of it. The Johnston ladies still dreamed of the heiress; a tall, lithe, dark woman with a deep contralto voice, they imagined her. She would be a banker's daughter, with a pursy father who would not appreciate her marrying a Sussex Johnston, but would infinitely prefer her to mate with a favourite clerk who might in time come in for a partnership. The old ladies felt that later the banker would relent, and come to appreciate the union. They talked about it among themselves in a lightly humorous vein that was uncomfortably serious. But Harley only thought of a plump, fair-haired confectioner's daughter of sixteen in Liverpool, with whom he imagined he was desperately in love, and to whom he used to write very bad poetry, modelled on some verses of Byron's, in which he found infinite solace.

HARLEY JOHNSTON, GENTLEMAN

At Oxford they took him out of the Eton jacket and swathed him in the folds of a gown, and taught him many things—leading him to differentiate between what is done and what is not done; what is due to a woman from a man; what is due from a man to himself and to other people. They took him in as the raw material of a gentleman, and by dint of the infinite patience the process requires, they turned him out a perfect product.

But at Oxford he developed tendencies that had never before been encountered in the Johnston family. He showed a leaning towards writing things. He had a few poems printed in a provincial magazine, and the editor of his home paper criminally encouraged him to the extent of giving him books to review. A short article in a revolutionary London weekly, and the disease was fully under way. The old ladies in Sussex were thunder-struck. Nothing like this had happened in the family as far back as living memory went. They were a little inclined to be shocked, as if Harley had proposed becoming an actor. There was no one they knew who wrote for a living, and they were not quite sure it was respectable. And then they remembered that Disraeli had written novels and that Mr. Balfour was the author of a volume of essays, and they were

HARLEY JOHNSTON, GENTLEMAN

somewhat reassured. And unquestionably there was a greater possibility of the heiress dream, for now Harley would of course go to London, and mix with the great world. Drilling grumbling infantrymen under the Burma sun, or scouring the China seas in a gunboat have their disadvantages when it is a question of making a rich marriage. Heiresses do not flourish in those localities. But in London, and for a poet, the matter was hardly difficult at all.

II

When we think of Fate, we imagine some great Power with distinctly human attributes, a Power that may hate an individual grimly and persecute him with all the cold fury of the Inquisition; or may help an individual in every possible way, showering opportunities within his reach, transmuting everything he touches into gold, like some beneficent household deity; or it may play with a man, as a cat plays with a mouse or a hawk with a sparrow before striking. It played with Harley Johnston.

First there came to the house in the Sussex downs the London paper that hinted at the insolvency of the little private bank in the Strand where all the

HARLEY JOHNSTON, GENTLEMAN

securities of the Johnston family were held, and the next morning came the letter confirming it. Bernhardi, that sleek, hook-nosed South African whom the threat of lynching had chased from the Transvaal, had diced with the money of soldiers' widows, and a thousand little homes in England, including the Johnstons', were to go beneath the hammer of the auctioneer, and their owners to live as best they could on the contemptuous charity of relations. In the Johnstons' case there was still enough left to keep the old ladies from absolute want, but no more Johnstons would wear the blue and gold of the navy, or the trim khaki of the "Buffs." There would be no income for Harley Johnston now. He would have to work for his living. If he could write, now was the time. Somehow the old ladies at home were glad that Harley had "the gift," as they called it, and saw in it the benevolent design of a Providence that no sooner closes one alleyway than it opens another. The way was open for Harley—the wind was tempered to the shorn lamb.

And then on the grey, gentle, old-world ladies, another blow fell. Their Dream became an impossibility. They had summoned him home in his triumph from the conferring of degrees, and had told him of the misfortune.

HARLEY JOHNSTON, GENTLEMAN

"Who knows?" his mother had said, "Harley may one of these days marry a girl with plenty of money, and retrieve all the family fortunes." She laughed pleasantly at the possibility.

"I am afraid not," Harley replied, with a little nervous smile.

"Why not, Harley? Goodness knows you're good-looking enough, and there are plenty of them to be found."

"Because," he began, and cleared his throat nervously, "I am engaged to be married to a girl who has none at all."

Her name was Claire Grahame, and she was twenty-one years old. She was fifth on the list of his amative adventures since the episode of the confectioner's daughter who had held his hand at a party. After the confectioner's daughter had come in turn the sister of a school chum, with wide black eyes, who had described his advances to her friends at length; then there had been a tall, black-haired sylph whom he had imagined sitting by his side and growing old with him after a life of achievement. She was followed by a plump, blonde barmaid to whom at least a dozen of his kind made calf-love every evening. The barmaid was in turn ousted by a widow in Brighton, who advised him kindly not to make a fool of himself. The ridiculous quality of these episodes came home to him in full force two minutes after he had met Claire Grahame.

He had gone home with a friend for a few weeks' visit after the Michaelmas term, and there he had met her. There was very little said at the first meeting. What impressed him most was the peculiar brown quality of the girl—brown wavy hair ruffled over the temples; brown eyes with little golden spots set in the pupils, and her tanned brown skin and hands. He had always felt uncomfortably shy with other girls, but with Claire Grahame young Johnston was ridiculously soon at his ease, and much astonished thereat. The first night he met her, he found himself, when he had left her, trying to remember the exact appearance of her face, and the next morning he felt an acute sense of anxiety lest she should not come down to breakfast. There had been a few tennis singles with her, a few rides along the country roads, a country ball where they had a couple of romping, laughing waltzes together, and then he had gone away. He remembered the difficulty he had in saying good-bye. They had stood together awkwardly, wanting to say something and not finding the words.

HARLEY JOHNSTON, GENTLEMAN

"I want to write to you," he managed to get out at last.

She nodded.

"Will you answer the letters?" he asked.

She nodded again.

"Well, good-bye," he said, and clattered down the terrace to the waiting dog-cart.

The letters began with reminiscences of the visit together; with solicitous inquiries regarding each other's health, and light comments on the news, and gradually merged into things that were watched for eagerly, and read agonizedly with futile efforts to get at the least hidden evidence of warmth between the lines. Then to both had come the keen desire to see each other again, and by dint of scheming, Harley succeeded in getting another invitation. This time they knew they were in love with each other. There were the usual long walks, the readings together, the delight at stolen moments when they slipped out to see each other for a few seconds. Then came the scared, awkward declaration on his part, and the timid acceptance of his love from her. And they had gone from each other that morning singing and weaving dreams of what the future would bring.

And then things had moved more quickly. They

each felt there was something more definite to be said than that they loved, so one evening, while the bittern boomed overhead and the night scent of the meadows rolled up to them, he took his courage in both hands.

"When I get my degree and find a berth, Claire," he asked, "will you marry me?"

In the shoulder of his tweed coat he thought he could hear her low "I will," and he hugged her closer.

III

Ability is something like the branch of a tree that ripens and becomes tough with the sun, the rain, and the passing of seasons. The young man imagines that he can fight his way through the world with a withe of sorrel wood; the man in his prime feels he can raise bruises with his stave of oak, and with his gnarled and seasoned cudgel the old man knows he can break heads. At twenty-three the world is our oyster, and we can open it with our knife, irrespective of whether the blade is made of Toledo steel or of Brummagem alloy. So Harley Johnston, acquainted with the wreck of the family fortunes, saw nothing more natural than that he should go out and mend them—something like the tiger cub which, having smelt blood, will go out and adventure for the nearest human within reach, not at all understanding that the human may carry in the crook of his arm a .404 Winchester that will vomit seven explosive bullets in three seconds.

At Oxford Harley had met Harrison, the Rhodes scholar from Delaware, a corpulent, clean-shaven, spectacled little man, with the optimistic quality of a bond salesman, who thought America, dreamed America, preached America.

"It is the country of the young man," he would reiterate, "it's there and there alone that the value of young blood is sufficiently understood. You don't have to wait until the man above you passes in his checks. If you've got the goods, they've got the money. Over here it's a funeral—over there it's a race, and the best man wins."

And Harley, who thought that when it came to racing he could cover one hundred yards in ten seconds, pondered deeply and long over the sermon of the Rhodes student. When you took his account of America in conjunction with the knowledge that Rudyard Kipling, Gouverneur Morris, and G. K. Chesterton get fifteen hundred dollars for each short story they write, the matter was absolutely startling. The ladies in Sussex saw nothing wrong with it. In place of the quiet Queen Anne red-brick-and-tiled house they had been dreaming of, they saw castellated spires rising in their imaginations —domains populated largely by footmen with prize-fighters' calves and the suave presence of diplomats.

To her credit be it said that the project did not appear so absolutely simple to Claire Grahame. While Harley soared to mansions on Fifth Avenue, she saw a four-roomed flat somewhere in the less costly districts of New York, which she would take care of while Harley was working. There was a great deal of planning for wedding arrangements, invitations, and the trip to New York. He would come over for her as soon as the career was well under way, which would hardly take more than six months. Then they would retire to the little flat. There was another long series of consultations over the furnishings of the home. They went over the whole matter in detail, papering and furnishing each of the rooms as they came to it, with a pretty and becoming embarrassment over the question of bedrooms and the like. There was no idyll in Theocritus to compare with theirs. In the cataclysmic failure of the bank they saw nothing but an act of God designed to give Harley a chance to prove himself, and the finger of a Providence that loved lovers pointing out the way to them where love would always flourish as in the warmth of the Sussex gloaming.

So, on a bright September afternoon when the sun was shining, Harley Johnston set forth to make his fortune. The old-world ladies stood prim and dignified on the pier with little pouches made by unshed tears showing puffed and purple beneath their eyes. They said very little, for they were of a race that has sent soldiers into battle in every generation and has seen few of them come back. And on the shoulder of one of them, the little brown girl was crying her golden-brown eyes out, her square shoulders shaking, her downy brown cheeks spangled with tears as with dew-drops. There was the hoarse, strident yell of the siren; a clatter and a rattle along the quay; a swirl of dark, slimy water about the pier and the figures that watched him faded from Harley Johnston's eyes as a slide fades in a magic lantern.

IV

It is peculiar that in every new-comer New York arouses the desire to conquer. The sight of the giant city lying, relaxed and lazy, like a cat, along the waterfront, brings out in the immigrant the lust of Attila as he gazed at Rome and her seven hills. Here is battle, here is victory, here is looting. Not until later do the tentacles of the city envelop them like the tentacles of a monster cuttle-fish, and even in defeat they have the memory of the first great moment when they saw New York as a ball to be tossed and juggled from hand to hand.

And so Harley Johnston saw it. To him it was Golconda, it was Canaan, it was the treasure city where the streets were of beaten gold from Ophir and the houses roofed with jade and jasper. He stood on the pier while the blue-uniformed, shrewd-eyed customs inspector rummaged suspiciously among his baggage, and he dreamed dreams in which he returned to the old-world ladies and the little brown girl laden down with riches and honour. To the baffled and dissatisfied customs man he was "a damned little cockney," but his visions were those of a Xenophon. Every street corner held for him a Don Quixote, where you and I only see a bum in a plug hat.

Days went by in a rush of hurrying visits, appointments, consultations with men who would hear him for courtesy, but who had nothing that would suit him. The few introductions he had soon gave out. It was a bad time in the year for him to have come, they said; why not have stayed in England? There were the usual rejection-deferring offers to "let him know if anything turned up," the usual tactfully worded or contemptuously brutal refusals of jobs. Money began running short. The days lengthened into weeks, and he removed from the modest hotel that had sheltered him to the seclusion of a rooming house on Thirty-fifth Street.

His letters to the little brown girl were, in the beginning, long, heavy epistles telling of his loneliness for her, recounting little incidents of their courtship with a "Do you remember?" making protestations of undying love and prophecies regarding the time they would be together in New York. There was a little irritation that things were not working out exactly as they had planned, but here he quoted the fact that it was a bad time of the year and though connections might be a little difficult to make there was no question of everything coming right in the end. Later on the letters became less sanguine, and there was more of the keen note of loneliness in them. Then there grew up a note that she recognized as anxiety. And later there came a touch of apathy that wounded her even more.

HARLEY JOHNSTON, GENTLEMAN

The days began to appear to him as a long, weary grind wherein he mounted stairs, flashed upward in elevators, accosted bustling and laconic office boys in vestibules, and saw or was refused an interview by earnest, tired men, who had much philosophy to offer and very little comfort. Occasionally there was a flash of hope that went out like a gutted candle in a few minutes. And then there was the visit to the next office varying only from the visit to the last in the manner of rejection. It had become like a duty that he couldn't shirk.

Pretty, on the *Era*, gave him something to think over.

"How many magazines, publishing houses, and newspapers have you visited in search of a job?" he asked.

"About forty-four."

"And they won't have you because you've no experience, are too young, they don't want anybody, and other reasons?"

"That's what they say it is," Johnston answered.

"Do you know what I would do if I were in your shoes?"

"I'd like to know what there is to do," Johnston said. "It seems to me I've done everything."

"I'd go home again. It's the best place for you.

HARLEY JOHNSTON, GENTLEMAN

I wouldn't stay in New York two minutes. It's the most dangerous city in the world for a man out of a job. Listen! Three years ago a young Irishman, better equipped than you are, came to me and asked for a place. We couldn't help him. A year ago I heard of him on the breadline. He's now in the Potter's Field—you know what that means. Listen again! After him there came a Cambridge man by the name of Notter. There was nothing for him either. To-day he's a hanger-on in the lowest opium den in Chinatown. Go over to Jim Davis on *Kennedy's*, or to Bob Holliday on the *Star*, and they'll tell you other things that are fifty times as bad as that. If you have got enough money to take you back, go next Saturday. If you haven't, work your way back on a cattle boat. Only don't stay here and play the game you're playing. It's hopeless. For God's sake go back before anything like that happens to you!"

And Johnson, the young fool, laughed!

HARLEY JOHNSTON, GENTLEMAN

V

If there is a street in the world that compares with any of the West Thirties in New York, it is the *Rue de Venise* in Paris. Both have the shame-faced look of a man who is a confirmed drunkard, cadger and crook, who is ashamed to associate with former friends and who dodges out of the way of meeting them. In the daytime the West Thirties have the dull, empty, apathetic appearance of sleeping off a debauch. By night they are spangled with bright, flashing spots where the painted hussies of the half-world walk slyly about in pinchbeck finery; where slim, effeminate youths with the waists of women, leer viciously at the passer-by; where the confidence man laughs his loud, brazen cackle and the wire-tapper waits for the unsuspecting countryman with the caution of the ferret; where the pickpocket wends his way in and out of the crowds on silent, nervous feet, and the whisky-thirsty bum attaches himself to strangers with his nervous, hunted, and inconceivably pathetic eyes. And there are dark spaces where the cocaine peddler waits for his customer as the flame waits for the moth,

HARLEY JOHNSTON, GENTLEMAN

where the cadet lurks to take her earnings from the street-walker, where dark, mysterious faces peer out with baffling questions unspoken and horrible invitations guessed at. Its colours suggest the iridescent shimmer on a sewer-pit, its dark places the pitch of the lowest of hells. Its denizens boast with pride that it is the worst place in the world—that Budapest cannot compete with its horrors, nor can Irkutsk, which Gorky once miscalled "the Snowy Virgin of the Steppes," nor can Buenos Aires, nor Vladivostok. There is no place on the green earth like it. It is Hell.

And here, in the innocence of his heart and his ignorance of the city, Harley Johnston from the green, sweeping Sussex downs, came to dwell. In a small hall bedroom up three flights of stairs, he placed photos of the Sussex ladies and of the brown-haired girl with the golden spots in her brown eyes. And here he came home evening after evening, broken, harassed, disappointed, to gain what strength he could from the pieces of inanimate pasteboard with the familiar faces on them. There were other little mementos of her there, too—her letters in a drawer; a handkerchief; a little knot of withered moss-roses she had given him one afternoon; a book of verse; other little fetiches of days that appeared to him sometimes like pages from a book he had read. Here he wrote his letters and planned for the morrow, and came back on the morrow night to plan with a little more apathy, with a greater sense of defeat, for the next day.

Of the inhabitants of the house he knew little or nothing. There was a clean-shaved, massaged man who passed him on the stairs every day with a muffled "Hello" whom he imagined was the true type of American business man, broker, bank official, or the like, but whom the police knew to be "Pete" Brady, agent for the Barcelona branch of the "Spanish Prisoner." There also he passed unwittingly "Sol" Freeman, unequalled in the art of placing counterfeit bills, and "Pop" Mulcahy, whose speciality was selling pawn tickets for pledged diamonds on Sixth Avenue, where he averaged one hundred and fifty dollars a week from the little mothers of Flatbush shopping in the afternoon. There also he met Larry Begbie, drunkard, "coke fiend," and star reporter for the *Universe*, who in five minutes told him more about the unspeakably obscene mysteries of New York than Harley had ever imagined of Nero's Rome. Begbie, perhaps from the newspaperman's carelessness, perhaps from a late feeling of delicacy or the fear of shocking the boy overmuch, refrained from telling him the nature of the roomers he housed with, and Harley still came home to the massive brownstone structure that looked like a palace beside its Chop Suey restaurant and dingy tailor's shop, with a feeling that he was returning to a home as austere, though peculiarly situated, as the forbidding, opulent residences on Fifth Avenue or the Drive.

There were other roomers there, too, whom he noticed, but in whom he felt little interest. There was a plump little blonde woman in furs, whom he often met coming down the steps with a Pekinese spaniel on a leash. She never spoke to him nor he to her. On his own landing, in a room across the corridor from his, another girl lived. He had caught a glimpse of her on one or two occasions when coming home early, and his memory registered the appearance of a tall, heavily built woman, with black hair and eyes, and a strongly marked mouth. She could hardly be over twenty-seven, he imagined, and he wondered why it was that she opened her door when he was coming up the stairs, and decided that she was waiting for someone. Once he met her on the stairs on an evening, and noticed that she was big and deep-chested and wore a modish hat and clothes that rustled as she moved. He put her out of his mind immediately, for men who have brown girls with golden spots in their brown eyes have little time to follow up fugitive speculations about other women. And usually he bounded up the stairs with a rush to see if by any chance there was a letter from the girl in his room, shaking the stairs until the other roomers jumped up with their hands to their hearts, wondering if by any chance some stiff-necked police inspector had been goaded by the commissioner into a clean-up of his precinct.

Daniel, they say, went into a den of lions, and emerged from it without a scratch or scar. Peter walked on the waves without wetting the soles of his sandals. The three Israelite children in captivity passed unharmed through the fiery furnace. Providence, it is explained, watched over them. But Providence wiped the name of Harley Johnston from its memory the day he walked up the steps of the brownstone house in Thirty-fifth Street.

VI

Another day had come and gone, and taken with it hopes, expectations and disappointments. There was to be a letter from Claire that night, but latterly those letters were beginning to irritate rather than to help him. There was so much confidence in them, such a spirit of waiting to hear of success, that he feared to read them as he would have feared to face the girl herself. It was to him as if she had placed future, hopes, comfort, and life in his hands, and that he was failing in the allotted task.

He let himself into the house, and as the key clicked in the latch he thought how easy it would be to take Pretty's advice and to go back home. He could get some little thing at home which after a few years would see them in comparative comfort, but that was not what he had been sent out for. There was too much dreaming in Sussex for him to go back; there had been too much blaring of trumpets. He had gone forth as men go forth to conquer far countries. He must either come home with booty or return on his shield.

The girl on his landing was coming down the stairs with her usual rustle and usual dignity, her big leather pocket-book clasped in her right hand. In the dim light of the hallway the faint breath of live scent struck the boy like a current of air. There was something alert, it seemed to him, about the jaunty cock of her hat, and something strong and powerful in the rigid setting of her shoulders and in the sweep of her walk.

Her arm struck against the banister as she turned into the hall, and the pocket-book dropped with a dull thud. He sprang forward and picked it up. He noticed she was looking at him with wide, black eyes.

"Thank you," she said, and he thought for the moment how her voice fitted in with the rest of her—deep, sonorous, and full like a bell.

"Not at all," he blurted out, and as he dashed up the stairs, he felt himself go red and hot to the roots of his hair. In her one brief glance it appeared to him that she had seen right through him, the pitiful little worries, disappointments and ambitions; the weak, clawing fight against fate; the puling puzzles.

He read the letters in his room with a twisted laugh on his face. There was one from Claire. She was sure that by this time he would have "news", that everything "had come right." News! Everything come right! Faugh! he jeered, if she only knew.

If she were only strong enough, he thought, he would tell her, but she was not that kind. She would think that he had failed if he told her how things were, and not understand that he had gone out on an errand that was pitifully foolish. How few women were strong, he smiled to himself; how few of them could face things as they really were. And then suddenly he thought again of the woman of the opposite room. There was something capable and big about her. He remembered the strongly marked mouth, the solid black line of eyebrow; the deep, unpuzzled eyes; the generous width of breast and shoulder, the high tilt of the head. There was something that could take blows and could deal them; not something to shiver before danger and run and whine in a corner.

Unconsciously he contrasted her with the girl at home who was waiting for him. Claire seemed to suggest the glint of spring and autumn sunlight, the clean breeze of the heath where the grouse called to the moorhen and brooks purled and the mavis chattered. The other woman suggested the strength and turmoil of the city, the blinding white light of great avenues and the dark, mysterious pools of ink of the side streets, or the blind alleyways where men battled to the death. The one was the cool, unruffled passage of a stream between meadows; the other the dark, strong undertow beneath bridges.

He felt with a sense of shock that he should not be contrasting the little girl at home with this woman of whom he knew nothing. There was something disloyal about it, something utterly shameful. He should not be thinking about the dark woman at all, he knew, and determined then and there to put her out of his thoughts as one would throw away the end of a cigarette. But she stole into his mind again unawares, creeping up like a landscape, when a mist breaks, slipping through his buttress of loyalty like a torpedo through a net. Her dark, inscrutable face rose up like an apparition, her eyes shot broadside glances at him from all corners of the little room; the red mouth with its strong, curving lines was always there to answer the question he felt rising within him.

He met her again that night. They happened to come up the steps of the house together and at her curt, formal greeting and the open glance of her eyes he felt a pain sear him across the chest and a fog rise before his eyes. As he fumbled with his latch key to open the door, feeling for the hole like a drunken man, she smiled again. There was something old, something cynically wise about that smile. Catherine of Russia wore it; it leered from the painted face of the Queen of Scots; it flashes on the mouth of Madame Elizabeth, on Da Vinci's antique canvas. It is the smile of the courtesan, of the painted harlot. The smile of woman defiled.

HARLEY JOHNSTON, GENTLEMAN

VII

Her name was Sally Tolliver. At eighteen she had left her village in Virginia with the trainer of a local racing stable, a bluff, squat, red-faced man in check riding clothes and with the hearty, easy manners of his kind, who promised to marry her when they got to Norfolk, but who then apprised her of a former and still existent union, and what was she going to do about it? And further, he pointed out, her own father was one of the sporting, racing fraternity and she herself the outcome of an equally uncomplicated union, and what the deuce had she got to kick about? So Sally Tolliver, being of a tribe that accepts the failure of the large issues in life as they accept the failure of the favourite to get past the post first, took the matter like a lost bet, and thought no more of it. Then followed a pleasant, varied tour of the race-tracks of America, where she learned the points of the sport of Life, how to win calmly and to lose gracefully, and laid the foundation of a broad philosophy that never failed her. There were three pleasant years amid the courtly tracks of Saratoga; the uproarious, shouting hordes of Sheepshead

HARLEY JOHNSTON, GENTLEMAN

Bay; the tense, shrewd sportsmen of New Jersey; the open-handed, rollicking Pacific Coasters; the soft-tongued, inconceivably cunning dwellers of New Orleans, and then the red-faced trainer lost his stake in the race of life, paid his bet like a sportsman and a gentleman, and left her alone in Buffalo.

Then there had been Schultz, the betting man, who had seen to her comfort until one day he confessed shame-facedly that he was going to be married, and had cried like an infant when she God-blessed him and wished him every luck. There had been Trelawny, the war correspondent who was now tracking northward to where the singing Frenchmen battled gallantly against the crushing, grim-mouthed Prussian lines. There had been Norton, the concert singer whom she had nursed through pneumonia, and sent back to his Tipperary home. There had been Billy, "Kid" Davis, whose smashing rush had put Papke out in the nineteenth round. All men, she said to herself and the tears came to her eyes; all big men, strong men, thank God! men whom it was good to be with.

And then there came the day when there was no one to take care of her for the time being, and she had to face the bleak prospect of the streets. The broad philosophy of the race track and the betting ring helped her out there. There were hard places in life for everyone, to be sure, but with the first touch of the frost there would be the south to turn to, with money enough for clothes, for train fares, for hotel bills, and there she was well known. There would be many a lover for Sally Tolliver, who was never known to go back on a man.

As for Harley Johnston, the little frightened pigeon who had wandered into a nesting place of hawks, she saw him as she saw many a man with a problem, baffled, harassed, and worn. Here was a little bit of life, and of life she was a connoisseur. She would help him if she could, and that she could she never doubted. There was only one way of helping a man that Sally Tolliver was aware of, and that was by loving him, and when she saw him shaking in a palsy of doubt, fear, and disappointment, she smiled. One can imagine the rather cynical, somewhat kind smile of a *deus ex machina* toward an individual in trouble. If the boy needed her, Sally Tolliver argued, he would come to her. If he came to her, she decided, she would help him. Not for money, not for passion, but for the indefinable pleasure it gave a woman like her to be of assistance to a man in trouble.

Which was all very well in its way, but was out of its orbit in this case. In Sally Tolliver's world

HARLEY JOHNSTON, GENTLEMAN

they fought the battle of life with honest staves that break bones and crack heads and raise weals that are black and blue. But broken bones can be set, and a physician can stitch together the opening in a split skull, and lotions and ointments remove the marks of bruises, and all is well again. But in Harley Johnston's world they fought the battle with long, slim duelling swords. A feint, a parry, and the steel was in a man's vitals to the hilt, and neither physician could help him, nor priest, nor philosopher.

VIII

Take a man in trouble. You and I are willing and glad to help him. It is our duty, our code, our creed. Let his trouble continue for a while. We are still willing and glad to help him, but after a time the spontaneous quality of our sympathy will not be there. We feel it is a duty. It grows irksome. Let his trouble still continue. You and I grow tired. It is high time for this meddlesome fellow to have a good story. Why must he always go around with a long face and a dreary word? We dodge down side streets when we see him coming. It's barbarous of us, unkind, unfeeling, but it is life. Some day we will both be in trouble, you and I, and we will have an opportunity of feeling the failure's end.

So when Harley Johnston became too importunate in his demands for a chance at different kinds of work, people refused to see him. They were busy, they said, and there was nothing doing. And Harley Johnston, who was sensitive, went out of the offices with a face exceedingly red, and a little empty feeling at the pit of his stomach. He muttered curses as he strode along the streets. The crowds flocking down Fifth Avenue became an army of enemies. Bitterness swelled up in his throat and poisoned him. Bitterness kept him awake at night and made his eyes red and hard when he rose in the morning. And there came a morning when he steadfastly refused to go out at all. There would be nothing for him but disappointments and rebuffs, anyhow, so he lay up in his room and dreamed little day dreams in which the gas bracket on the wall figured, and then the East River, and then the rush of an incoming subway train. And then there came a day in which he pitched unread the letter of the little brown girl in Sussex into the waste paper basket with a laugh that was more than half a sob.

He had been everywhere where there was work

HARLEY JOHNSTON, GENTLEMAN

to be had. He had not baulked at physical labour, but there was little to do in that line for even the hardy Italian or the muscular negro, and the foreman of a gang is not keen to hire anyone whose finger-nails are pared. A day or two trying to sell subscriptions for a magazine and failing miserably smashed him altogether. A sort of shame came over him that in a world of workers there was no place for him.

He wondered how the girl on the landing had come to know that he was looking for a job. Three days ago, as he was going out, she had opened the door of her room and asked him to bring her in some magazines, and twice since then she had met him on the stairs as he was coming in.

"Any luck?" she had asked cheerily.

"Not yet," he had answered, as if she knew the ins and outs of the case, and then he puzzled how she had understood. He wondered if she knew any of the people to whom he had applied for work; there was no other way for her to have known, he said to himself—as if it weren't evident to everyone in the droop of his shoulders, in the haggard look in his eyes, in the tired plod of his step.

There came over him a great want of sympathy from some one. The feeling that of all the five million souls in the city no one wanted him, cared for him, knew of him, swept through him like a storm. The pathos of his setting out, like Launcelot, in quest of the Grail, struck him like a blow. There was no one he could tell of it; he couldn't confess it to the little brown girl, who thought of him as a champion in armour, or to the fragile, gentle ladies at home, who knew nothing of the stress and strain of battles in cities. There was no one to whom he could go. Tears welled up in his eyes and flowed over.

There was a low, firm knock on the door, and she stood there, tall, broad, imperial, with her hair massed low on her brow, her right hand holding up the folds of her dress.

"If you are going out," she said, "I wonder if you would mind very much doing something for me—mailing a letter."

He got his hat and coat and followed her out into the hall. She moved toward her room.

"I have just to put the address on it. Won't you come in and wait a moment?"

He followed her into the room, and sat down and looked around him while she wrote. He noticed the spacious lines of it compared to his own meagre domicile. There was a green rug on the floor, with a big square couch. Along the wall were a smaller

HARLEY JOHNSTON, GENTLEMAN

couch, a screen that hid a wash-stand, a bookcase full of books and magazines, a table with more magazines and a reading lamp, a couple of comfortable chairs, and the little polished desk where she was writing. A few watercolours dotted the walls, and a curtain hid a closet that bulged with clothes. There was a great sense of comfort about it, a sense of someone's home.

"You've got a very comfortable place here," he said. He wanted to hear her voice again.

She rose and handed the letter to him. He felt a gasp swell within him as he looked at her, as might a swimmer who sees the sweep of a giant wave in the distance.

"Yes, it is comfortable," she was saying. "Your own little place across the hall is rather cramped. But we can't always have what we want, can we? Well, thank you for mailing the letter, Mr.—"

"Johnston is my name."

"Mr. Johnston. My name is Tolliver. You haven't been long in New York; isn't that so?"

"Hardly more than two months."

"How do you like it?" she asked. "Do you know many people here?"

"I don't like it very much," he answered, "and I don't know a living soul in the whole city."

HARLEY JOHNSTON, GENTLEMAN

"Well, any time you feel lonely and like a chat, drop over here. I know very few people myself, and I'll be glad to see you."

There was something dumbfounding about it, something wonderfully unexpected. To sit in this well-lighted, comfortable room for an hour, instead of in his own cramped cubby-hole, and to talk with this big, capable woman! The boy's eagerness made his voice tremble.

"I should simply love to. When may I come?"

"Drop in to-night if you wish. I shall be at home all evening.

His spirits bounded as he went down the stairs, and his step took on the firm, springy ring it had before he began on his hopeless march around the offices. For a moment it occurred to him that it was not right for him, a man engaged to the little brown-haired girl three thousand miles away, to be sitting of an evening in the room of a strange woman of whom he knew nothing and who knew nothing of him. There was no harm in it, he said to himself, it was nothing but friendly, companionable, what might be expected to happen in this strange new country where men and women played, fought, and worked side by side. He felt nothing for her but thanks for her kindly offer to keep him from loneliness awhile. There was nothing wrong with it; nothing that Claire mightn't know or that he couldn't tell to the Sussex ladies.

And then there came to him the line of the firm, strong mouth, and the bulk of the splendid, pillar-like throat, and the depth of shoulder and bosom. He remembered the twinkle of her shoes on the stairway, and the swinging outline of her figure when she walked. These came into his head unbidden, like wreaths of smoke curling up from a fire, and remained with him whenever he spoke, read, or thought. And then one instant he remembered a white glimpse of shoulder he had caught through her wrap the day she asked him to bring the magazines, and he gasped suddenly as if he had received a blow full in the chest.

IX

He went the round of old rebuffs and disappointments that day, mounted in the same elevators, waited in the same offices, sent in the same requests and received the same curt or courteous refusals. He didn't seem to mind them, for they were little if at all in his mind. He decided that he would call on her about eight o'clock and every few minutes

HARLEY JOHNSTON, GENTLEMAN

he looked at his watch and reckoned up the hours between. Sometimes he would feel a heavy weight upon his chest, as if he were about to embark on a great adventure. At other times he felt a sense of great elation, as if he were about to receive great pleasure. The slowness of time passing roused him to a pitch of feverish impatience.

At eight o'clock he knocked at the door and walked in. The room was as he had seen it in the morning, but there was a keen sense of warmth in it, and an atmosphere of creamy light. She was sitting in an arm-chair as he entered, and when she rose he thought how well the light brought out the mature lines of her face and silhouetted the full curves of her figure. The loose, swirling muslin dress she wore sat on her like the vestment of a priestess. The wide ease of the room, the mellow light, and she herself, all suggested to him an harmonious chord struck by a master musician.

They talked on. A little bit about the weather, a little bit about New York, something of England, something of Broadway and Fifth Avenue. It seemed to the boy that they were sparring like boxers, waiting for the moment to send home a telling blow. A sense of nervousness came over him. Once he felt like jumping up and running off.

HARLEY JOHNSTON, GENTLEMAN

"Had any luck to-day!" she asked, suddenly.

"Oh, none," he answered, "same old thing every day. By the way, how did you know I was looking for work?"

"Oh, I know," she replied and the slow, wise smile broke again on her face. "There are a good many things I know."

He wished she hadn't brought that up. The old feeling of bitterness came over him. His eyeballs hardened like stone. The terror of failure and despair gripped him anew like paralysis. In the distance a clock chimed nine brazen strokes.

He wanted to say something, but he couldn't find words. He put a cigarette in his mouth and fumbled in his pockets for a match. There was a box on the reading table beside her. He went over and picked it up.

"Do you mind?" he asked.

"No, I like it." She was looking up at him. His fingers trembled as he lit the cigarette. There was a haggard look on his face, and the lines around his mouth set into a grim triangle.

"Yes," he said aloud to himself, "work's a hard thing to get. By God, it is!"

"Sit down," he heard her say, "sit down and tell me about it." She pointed to the arm-chair beside her.

HARLEY JOHNSTON, GENTLEMAN

"Oh, there's nothing much to tell," he said with a laugh. "Ordinary thing, I suppose." He sank into the arm-chair and looked at her. Her eyes were fixed on him. There seemed to be something in them that understood. He began the story of confidence, hope, and disappointment from the day he passed from the quiet dock to the hustling streets of Manhattan. His lip quivered. His hands knotted together like pieces of steel mechanism, and he winked his eyelids once or twice and squared his jaw.

The quiet of the room fell upon him like a balm. It seemed to him that he was throwing ropes off that had bound him until now, and that he was being freed. The face of the woman opposite had the grave immobility of the Theban Sphinx. His own voice droned on like the chanting of a priest. The strokes of the chimes on Fifth Avenue rang in like a portion of a ritual.

"I suppose I was a fool to come over," he ended dully, "I suppose I was a fool to come."

He felt suddenly that he was going to break down He rose, walked around a few steps and sat down on the couch.

"I shouldn't have worried you like this," he faltered. "It wasn't fair. But you seemed to understand; it was rotten of me."

HARLEY JOHNSTON, GENTLEMAN

He buried his face in his hands. A sob broke through like the explosion of a gun. And suddenly she was sitting beside him with her arm around his shoulder.

"That's all right," she was saying, "I know. I know all about it."

He was crying outright now. Both arms went around him. She stroked the back of his head, his face, his eyes.

"Poor kid," she murmured, "poor kid. It's been tough."

The sobbing ceased little by little. He smiled at her through moist eyelids. She bent down suddenly and kissed him. A shiver went through him like a fever.

The thought of Claire Grahame flashed into his mind like a picture on a cinematograph. It seemed to urge him to break the arms from around him, and to escape. He put it out of his mind as a drowning man lets go his clutch of a spar.

The arms went more closely about him. Kisses fluttered on his forehead and eyes like drops of cooling water. The faint odour of scent went to his head like alcohol. There was a sense of warmth and a sense of softness. Kisses seared his mouth like live flame.

A clock in the distance struck two, like beats on

a bass drum. Good God! was it as late as that? How could it be? It was nine only a few minutes ago.

"I must be going," he said, "I mustn't keep you up." But he felt he could make no movement to go.

"Poor boy, he doesn't want to go . . ." he heard her murmur.

A feeling of intoxication swept over him, a feeling of unconsciousness. It flowed about him in warm, swirling waves. Beside him he could hear her murmur like the rustle of leaves.

"He doesn't want to go . . . Well, then, he shan't. . . ."

X

Consider man—a highly complicated agglomeration of reasoning power, sensitiveness, and emotional quality; a being who in nine cases out of ten believes in and works toward a future existence, Abraham's Bosom, Heaven, the Bower of Allah, Nirvana, or whatever his choice may be. He has codes of honour, rules, beliefs, and other weapons to protect him on the trail. You and I, for instance, are men. Put you or me on Monday in some village of the Congo; by Wednesday we will lash the back of any native who fails to get out of our way quickly; on Saturday we will cut the tongue out of an unfortunate servant

HARLEY JOHNSTON, GENTLEMAN

who lies to us. Let us have acute rheumatism. We are given one, two, three hypodermic injections of morphine, and in three months time we will plead with slatternly negresses to sell us tablets of heroin; we will steal to get it; cut throats for it. We are the human, sentient, emotional being called man.

There was more agony for Harley Johnston the morning after he had visited Sally Tolliver than the weeks of disappointment had caused him. Before the night was done, he knew what she was—scarlet woman and harlot, they would call her at home, with the brutality of well-bred women. All day long he had sat with clenched hands and glaring eyes at the thought of it. What about Claire? What about his women-folk at home? There was no going back now. There never could be. He would throw himself in front of a subway train, he would dive headlong from Brooklyn Bridge. What was there left for him now?—he was unclean, like an old time Israelite whom a leper had touched. And then she opened the door of his room, and he fluttered into her arms like a tame pigeon.

A week slid by on rapid, pattering feet. There were no more thoughts of the swirling current of the river or the grinding wheels of the train. Thoughts of Sussex and the Surrey hills had faded away like forgotten verses. The vision of the tall, dark woman who loved him was before his eyes morning and night. There was something splendid about her, something regal. It lit a warm glow about his heart that healed the scars of battle and made him indifferent to the refusals and rebuffs of Park Row. He was a man, he said to himself; he had proved it.

Another week. The raffle of the city had still brought him no successes. Old bitterness was coming back. He thought of the brown girl in England with hard contempt—if she hadn't been the light-weight, the weakling she was, he might have done something. If she had only been like this strong, passionate woman who understood and who sympathized and to whom he could go in trouble, there would have been no question of defeat. He would have won.

For by now he admitted he had made a hash of it. There was no one to work for, no star to look up to; no future to aim at. He had an appointment with an editor downtown that afternoon on the very slim chance of getting something, but he felt it would be like all the rest of the applications.

"Ah, to hell with him!" he snarled. He wouldn't go. He threw himself back and lit a cigarette.

So Circe's herd of swine contented themselves

HARLEY JOHNSTON, GENTLEMAN

with plucking blades of clover and rooting for acorns in her magic forest, and forgot how they once had been leaders of armies—champions on horseback, fighting-men in armour.

XI

One borrows first from one's friends in large sums, then in small ones. One borrows then from acquaintances—"a dollar for car-fare, for a telegram, for a friend," and slips around the corner to the tiled dairy lunch. Then comes the sinister stuffiness of the pawnshop, where one waits nervously while the swarthy, shrewd-eyed attendant squints contemptuously at the pledges one offers. Then the books go, for a quarter, for a dime, for a nickel. Then one waits for a miracle, like the ravens of Elijah, or the manna in the desert, and tries to convince one's self that people do not die for want of food.

Watch and chain, clothes, portmanteau and books had gone from Harley Johnston, and at last the day came when at six o'clock he found himself debating whether to spend his last nickel on cigarettes, a glass of beer, or pitch it into the gutter. And after that, what? he asked himself.

The door opened and Sally Tolliver walked in, drawing on her gloves.

HARLEY JOHNSTON, GENTLEMAN

"Going out to dinner, boy?" she asked.

"Not yet, Sally."

"Why aren't you? You always go out about this time, don't you?"

"I don't feel like it to-night. I think I'll wait awhile."

She looked at him narrowly through slitted eyelids. He was getting red and uncomfortable.

"Have you got any money?" she asked shortly.

"Tons of it."

She waited a moment. He felt the crimson creeping from his eyebrows to his hair.

"Look here, young one," she said, "I don't believe you've got a red cent."

"Of course I have, Sally. I've got plenty left."

He felt her catch his right hand and thrust something in it. He tried to wrench it away.

"Now, look here, kid," she was saying, "don't be silly. You can give it to me back when you've got it. It's only a loan. Don't make me mad. Take it and have done with it."

She flashed out of the door with a swirl. He looked at the crumpled bill in his fingers. He would put it in her room. It was impossible to take it. The thought that she even had offered it seemed to crush him to earth like a heavy weight. He would put it back in her room before going out. He could do without it. Something was sure to turn up. Something always did.

Twenty dollars. The price of room-rent, dinners and breakfasts; the chance of redeeming the meagre pledges. If only a man had offered it to him, the sense of relief, the sense of power, it would give him. But to take it from a woman, from Sally Tolliver, who got it—he shuddered.

Something might turn up, but if something didn't, and God knows he had waited long enough for it, what would he do? To-night he would be hungry, to-morrow stupid, to-morrow night on the breadline, the next day huddling with the derelicts in Madison Square, reading scraps of newspapers, eyeing the Italian bootblack murderously as he pocketed the nickels of patrons. And around the corner was Henry's little place, where suave Sicilian waiters shuffled up and down the aisles and the band played the dreamy music of Strauss. He stuffed the bill into his pocket with an oath. After all, it was only a loan from friend to friend. He would pay it back as soon as things turned, and they were bound to turn sometime. It was little compared to what he would do for Sally if she ever needed it and he were able. He caught up his hat and dashed down the stairs.

But nothing turned up, and a week later the same

scene occurred, and it occurred again later. The second time there was a little less reluctance, a little less self-disgust, and a little more confidence as to the final paying back of it. The third time it was hardly more serious than a loan from a man friend.

He gave up the round of visits to the offices where he had been told to drop in now and again. Some of the places had his address and if anything did turn up, he argued, they would let him know. He had given up writing home—whenever he did get fixed, he thought, he would cut away from where he was staying and take up things where he had let them drop, giving some satisfactory reason for his silence. The letters from the little brown girl had ceased. When he had stopped opening them, and had not written, God knows what she thought. Perhaps she had visions of Harley in the arms of a Fifth Avenue heiress, whom he had entranced with his charms, and who would marry him willy-nilly. At any rate she cried very bitterly, and thought of herself romantically as the maiden with a handsome lover who had kissed and had ridden away. And the little old-world ladies asked each other with frightened eyes what Harley was doing that he did not write, and invented many fond and pathetically ridiculous excuses to account for it.

HARLEY JOHNSTON, GENTLEMAN

XII

What Harley was doing was very far from what the old ladies imagined, very far from what the little brown girl imagined, very far from what he himself would have thought a scant five months before. Harley was lying abed in the mornings, rising to go yawning to the mail, sauntering out to pass each day as best he might until the next would come. Harley's day was spent mostly about the dingy, debauched restaurants of Sixth Avenue, where the shifty-eyed dwellers of the locality lazed through late breakfasts and suppers and scowled at each other with hot, suspicious eyes; in the bar-rooms of the Thirties, dawdling over sogging glasses of beer, and rubbing elbows with the cadets and bullies of Eighth Avenue; in the cheap cabarets of the neighbourhood, where reckless, intoxicated women from the suburbs tangoed with the dregs of New York; in the mysterious, unspeakably evil Chinese restaurants near the river, where ginseng mixed with the Oriental dishes drugged those past the effects of ether and cocaine; in the vile and dangerous dance-halls of San Juan hill, where fallen white men writhe through tortuous measures with debased coloured women. These he searched for amusement, for forgetfulness, for something to pass the hours away.

He seemed to have forgotten what he had come to America for and what he had been. Once or twice he remembered Pretty's advice with a shiver and put it from him with a curse. One afternoon as he went down Sixth Avenue he caught sight of Pretty walking toward a tube station, and he bolted down a side street like a rabbit.

There was still the occasional bill from Sally, given always under the guise of a loan, and handed out and accepted now without the first embarrassment of offer and refusal. And somehow lately he was coming to hate the girl for giving it to him, and for having to go to her for it. She herself, he noticed with a suspicious eye, was not half so eager to give it. She had begun by urging him toward harder efforts to get work and to justify himself by achievement, but now she hardly ever spoke of that. He wondered with a dull surge of anger if she, too, thought that he was good for nothing, that there was nothing in him to make good with.

He hurried out in the mornings and around the bars to meet men he had become acquainted with, shifty crooks of the neighbourhood who liked his company for the class from which he had sprung,

HARLEY JOHNSTON, GENTLEMAN

and whose society he enjoyed because of their enmity to the people whom he considered had wronged him. There was "Slim" Aleck Brady, sometime cadet, sometime pickpocket, who had risen in the ranks of the underworld until now he did "talk work" in the robbing of jewellers' shops. There was "Kid" Devlin, gangster and politician, who supplied repeaters on election day at so much per head. There was Canton Louie, tout for hop layouts. Sometimes he became conscious of the degradation of the men he was with, and broke back to his hall bedroom with flaming cheeks and quivering muscles, in an agony of self-accusation. And then in a few hours, thoughts and memories would creep in on him like the ghosts of murdered men, and he would dash out again to meet someone and to talk to him, anything to keep the thoughts away. There was no one else he knew; he had to go back to the gunman and the opium tout.

He was beginning to drink, too. Night after night there were highballs of purple rye until he rose in the morning with a head that hammered like a mechanic's shop, and throat raw and itching. He would dash into the bar for a drink in the morning before breakfast.

There came the morning when he rose with the

same itch in his throat and fierce throbbing at his temples. He dressed to go out, and started down the stairs. His hand went into his pockets and came out with a start. He had forgotten. He had spent his last cent the night before.

He stopped and went up the stairs again mechanically. He would have to ask Sally for another loan. He hated to do that. It would be the first time he himself had broached the subject. He opened the door of her room and walked in with flushed face and twitching lips.

She was sitting in front of the little dressing table when he entered, polishing her finger nails with long, sweeping strokes of the buffer. She turned halfway around and looked at him. He noticed with a sense of shock that the kindly light had gone from her eyes. What he saw in them now was a sort of tolerant contempt.

"Well," she asked, "what can I do for you this morning?"

He couldn't bring himself to the point of asking for the money. He felt he hated her for not offering it.

"I just dropped in," he faltered.

She caught his eye for a moment, and his gaze dropped.

"Had any breakfast yet?" she asked.

HARLEY JOHNSTON, GENTLEMAN

"No," he said, "I didn't get out yet."

She opened the drawer of the dressing table and took out a bill. She reached it toward him with a long sweep of the arm.

"I suppose that's what you're after," she said, with a light laugh. "Take it, like a good boy, and run off. I'm busy to-day."

The edge of the bill seemed to sear his fingers. He felt he ought to pitch it out of the window.

"Thanks awfully, Sally," he tried to put a bluff heartiness into his voice. "I'll let you have it back just as soon——"

"Oh, for heaven's sake, stop!" she cut in. "You don't have to pull that all the time."

He slunk out as if he had been lashed along the flanks with a whip. Blood pounded in his head as he swallowed his drink in the bar, as he gulped down breakfast in the dingy restaurant. To be spoken to like that by a woman of the streets, he, Harley Johnston! Had he fallen as low as this?

He lunged out of the restaurant and into a saloon next door. He needed a drink, many drinks, to pull him together that he might think this over and decide what to do. The bar was filled with the early morning rush of Tender-loin dwellers. Clean-shaven, pink-faced men hung thoughtfully over whisky glasses and siphons. Slender, flashily-dressed youths dawdled by the ticker. Here and there a man volleyed out with a ringing, brazen laugh. There were many he knew there; Larry Baker, who operated for purses around the lobbies of the Broadway hotels; Mike Sullivan, who was the bodyguard of "Gentleman Jim" Smith, seller of morphine; "Lefty" Mack, gunman and gangster, while along the bar rail lounged the huge bulk of Pete Connor, dean of the bogus real estate men, whom Johnston knew by sight but had never spoken to. The boy edged in beside him, and called for a drink. He turned around to Connor.

"What'll you have?" he asked.

The towering body of the master crook swung around as if on an axis.

"What's that you're saying?" he asked.

"Will you have something to drink?"

Connor looked at him with cold, contemptuous eyes.

"I may be a crook," he began, and every word bit like acid; "I may be a con man, but by God! I don't drink with cadets."

It seemed to strike him like a blow in the face. A cadet! A parasite on the women of the underworld! Good God! He staggered away from the

HARLEY JOHNSTON, GENTLEMAN

bar, and pushed out unseeing through the swinging panels of the door. A cadet! He stumbled toward Fifth Avenue like an animal that has been wounded in the vitals and is looking for a place in which to die.

XIII

It was wintry on the avenue—a cold, whipping breeze and the promise of frost by night. Trim, fashionable women walked briskly along the pavement, looking neither to the right nor left. Tall, well-groomed men swung along, tapping at their thighs with canes or swinging them carelessly to and fro. Taxies clattered excitedly past. Graceful, purring limousines slid up to or away from the pavement. Occasionally a dogcart went spanking by, and at short intervals the huge green motor-buses lumbered along like Juggernauts.

Harley Johnston made an effort to collect himself as he turned the corner into the avenue. He wanted some place to think, to puzzle out what to do, if there was anything at all he could do. Thoughts, emotions, sensibilities seemed to weave in and out of each other like the pattern on a loom. He wanted to marshal them all into proper order so that he could review them with a single glance. The insult of the Sixth Avenue crook had acted on him like a splash of water in the face of a sleeper. It had brought him to himself with a paralysing shock.

He walked up the avenue toward Forty-second Street. A few men and women turned and looked at him as he passed by. The trim suit cut close to the body, the stick and spats proclaimed him the Englishman. But why, some of them asked themselves, was his face flaming as if it had been struck lately, and why that staring, hypnotized look in his eyes?

At Fortieth Street he stopped short. What was there to do? He gazed dully at the squat expanse of the Library, as if he expected it to answer. What was he to do?

"I beg your pardon!"

He wheeled around suddenly, and then nearly reeled and fell. A girl, dressed in a trim, tailored suit of blue serge, with a small three-cornered velvet hat and a white scarf about her throat, faced him. He had thought for a moment it was Claire. The clear cut features and chiselled profile reminded him of her. But Claire was brown as a berry, and this girl was fair.

"I'm afraid I startled you," she said, "I'm awfully sorry."

HARLEY JOHNSTON, GENTLEMAN

"That's all right," he answered, as he fumbled for his hat. "Can I help you?"

"If you wouldn't mind directing me to the Plaza—it's at Fifty-ninth Street, I think?"

Her accent and the clear-cut, bitten-off words suddenly brought London to his mind; the dull roar of the Strand, the tall pillar in Trafalgar Square, the Tower clear-cut against the sky like an etching.

"If you are walking up," he ventured, "I'll be glad to show you the way. I am English, too. My name is Harley Johnston."

"Thank you very much—if it doesn't bring you out of your way. My name is Wyckoff, Ethel Wyckoff."

They turned and walked northward. Something seemed to open in Harley Johnston's mind, and let in old memories and old feelings. The fierce, gripping nightmare of the last months passed away in a mist, the figures in the rooming-house, in the bars and cabarets slid out of his thoughts like phantasms that had no real existence. He was once more among people he knew, hearing sounds to which his ear was attuned, surrounded by the fashions and trappings of his old life. He drank in the sound of her voice and the trivial small talk as a dying man takes in draughts of air. He didn't care what she talked about; he only wanted to hear her speak.

HARLEY JOHNSTON, GENTLEMAN

Things were already becoming clearer. It was like the strains of David's harp banishing the evil vision of Saul.

"I am a governess over here," she explained. "I'm glad I asked you the way. It's so good to meet any one from home. Do you feel that?"

He felt like taking her by the arm and shouting aloud to her that it was salvation to him, that it was food and drink to a starving man, that it was a ray of sunlight to one in an oubliette.

"Yes," he answered, "it's awfully good."

They were passing the Cathedral now. In the distance the square at Fifty-ninth Street loomed like an oasis.

"Are there many Englishmen over here?" she asked.

"A good few."

"I meet very few of them," she said. "How do they make out?"

Something flashed into his mind like the spark of a wireless. He would put the matter up to her as to an umpire.

"Some of them well," he began, "some of them not so well. Some of them find nothing to do, and go to the dogs through drink and drugs." He took a deep breath. "One of them I know is like that. He is down in the depths of degradation. There is no help for him. The lowest crook in New York despises him. What are you to do in a case like that?"

He felt as if he had pleaded "Guilty," and were awaiting sentence.

"What can he do?" she seemed to blaze out at him. "If things are as bad as that he can end them. He can take a pistol and blow out his brains like a gentleman."

"Yes," he answered slowly, "yes, he can do that. He can always do that, can't he?"

He felt as if the red judge on the bench had put on the little black skull cap, and that the jury in their box had blenched to the colour of lime.

They were by this time standing opposite the big hotel. She turned around and faced him with blue, unclouded eyes.

"I liked the walk immensely. It was awfully good," she smiled.

"I enjoyed it, too," he answered gravely. "It meant a good deal to me."

"Thank you ever so much for showing me the way." She put out her hand. "Good-bye. I may see you again some day."

"I am afraid," he answered as he took the hand, raised the gloved fingers, and kissed them in full sight of the square, "that you never will."

HARLEY JOHNSTON, GENTLEMAN

XIV

Well, then, the issue was clear-cut, and the little girl had given judgment. He would end it. He would take this life of his that he had made such a patchwork mess of, and pitch it away, as a journeyman throws away a botched piece of work. What was there for him? He could never go back to the brown girl in Sussex or to the clean-souled gentle-women of his household with that black stain on him. He had been a cadet; he had lived on the money of a woman of the streets. The leper in his lair would shudder at the defilement of such as he.

He would take his life in both hands and throw it away. Not because of despair, not because of fear of life, but because it was a foul thing, like the clothing of one dead of the plague. His step took on a spring, his shoulders went back like those of a soldier on parade. He would pay for his offence. What did they say? "If thy right hand offend thee, cut it off." His whole life was a walking, living offence, and he would cut it in two, as a knife shears through rope.

He would go back to the rooming-house and burn the letters and papers there, and decide how he would do it. He must drop out quietly and secretly, he thought, and bring no scandal on the Sussex home. He thought for a moment of the little girl in her garden and the gentle shadows of the women at home, and a sense of oppression gripped him in the throat. Then he pulled himself together and walked onward.

He had turned in along Central Park, and was striding west toward Broadway. A boy dashed past him, running at full speed. He noticed people looking backward from a passing surface car. What was wrong? he wondered. Away in the distance he could hear the frenzied hooting of a fire-engine's siren, and the throbbing notes of a bell. The rattle of horse's hoofs sounded like the faint roll of a drum. Men appeared running from all directions. He gathered himself up and raced forward with them.

They cut across the Circle and into Sixtieth Street. He could see, halfway down the block, smoke swirling upward in sinister black clouds. Here and there a tongue of scarlet licked against the black like a splash of red ink. A hook-and-ladder team tore around the corner with a clatter and crash, and the crowd swirled violently against the line of police. He dived into it head foremost.

"What is it?" he heard some one ask, "a private house?"

HARLEY JOHNSTON, GENTLEMAN

"Private house nothin'." There was a snicker and a laugh. "Don't you see the girls on the street?"

He tore his way through the mob like a footballer through a scrum and pierced into the edge. Before him was a wide circle dabbled with little pools of water and interlaced with hosepipes. On one side a group of slatternly women in bedraggled finery clung together in terror, and gazed with open, staring eyes at the burning brownstone house. Firemen in helmets and rubber coats hurried out, dragging furniture and throwing it carelessly on the sidewalk. There was a dull crash, and a shower of sparks from the roof shot upward.

The police began pushing the crowd back. A fireman staggered through the door, swayed from side to side, and crashed forward down the steps.

"Get back there! Do you want the stick?" Harley got a blow in the ribs from the giant policeman in front of him. "The house is going to fall in a minute. Get back!"

"Are they all out?" he heard a bystander ask.

"Yeh," the policeman drawled tiredly, "all out hours ago."

The pall of smoke wavered and parted. He could see a window faintly through the mist. There seemed to be something behind it beating feebly at the pane. He touched the policeman on the arm.

HARLEY JOHNSTON, GENTLEMAN

"Look up there!" he shouted, "there's someone at the third story window. Don't you see it?"

The huge Irishman looked up indulgently.

"You're seeing things, son," he laughed. "Didn't I tell you they was all out?"

"I tell you there is!"

"Well, I tell you there's not! And if there is, there's no way out now. So whoever it is has got to stay there."

"What's one of them more or less, anyhow," someone remarked behind him with a laugh. "There's not such a want of them."

The cloud wavered and parted again. Again he thought he could see the white blur at the window. Good Heavens! wasn't there anybody to see it but himself? and if there were somebody there, was no one to attempt a rescue?

A message ticked into his brain, as another had come to him when walking up Fifth Avenue with the little English girl. Here was something for him to do before the curtain dropped on his tragedy. His sacrifice might help someone. He might replace one life with another, return new lamps for old.

He stripped off his overcoat and edged in a few inches more. It was hardly forty yards to the steps. The policeman turned aside for a moment and he dashed forward.

HARLEY JOHNSTON, GENTLEMAN

He heard a dull roar behind him as the mob saw him race. He leaped over a network of hose and dodged a charging fireman. He was on the steps now. Heat struck at him like the blast of a furnace. A hand clutched at his shoulder. He wrenched away and sprang through the door.

Smoke rolled over him in huge, liquid waves. It seemed to pour down his throat like water, and to clog his footsteps. He fumbled for the banisters and began dragging himself upward. Heat shrivelled his skin like the live flame of a blowpipe. He reached the first landing with a stagger and clawed his way on. A shower of sparks struck him like the points of needles. There was a loud, staccato rattle, like the volleying of musketry, and a thunderous roar like the crash of great ordnance.

He knew he wanted to get upstairs to where the figure in white beat its futile tattoo against the window pane. Pictures ran in and out of his head like the reel of a bioscope. First there was the vision of the girl in Surrey creeping in under his shoulder, and looking up at him in trust and love. And then the group around the trellised home in Sussex, spinning day dreams in which he centred as hero, and protector, and saviour. And then arose the dark vision of Sally Tolliver, with head thrown back and arms outstretched toward him, and the hell-hounds of Sixth Avenue crowding behind like a pack of hunting dogs. And then there came himself, crouching like a quarry whom the hunters have at bay, looking everywhere for a loophole of escape. And lastly came the fair girl of Fifth Avenue, who pointed out to him a loophole through a dark gully, beyond which he could see in the distance green hills and the sun shining and the glint of the open sea.

He was on the second landing now. Red flame stabbed at him from corners and followed him as he struggled on. There was a fierce smarting along his side and his eyeballs burned like hot coals. He felt the sinews of his throat crack like bursting wood.

He was on his way, he knew, through the gully that had been pointed out to him. At any moment he would break into the green fields. He seemed to hear voices. There was the voice of the fair girl urging him on, telling him that at the end Claire would be waiting for him, and the voice of Sally Tolliver, whispering to him to come back to where was warmth and scented beauty, and the merry tunes of dance halls, and the cosy companionship of bars. And then there came the voice of his father, telling the men to stand firm by their guns, and he braced like a charger.

HARLEY JOHNSTON, GENTLEMAN

The banister gave under his hands like pasteboard, and he reeled crashing through a door. He staggered to his feet again. There was a window through which light struggled in a mist of muddy brown, and there on the floor was a limp, white bundle that he knew was what he had come for. He dragged it forward and smashed at the window with great heaves of shoulder and chest.

Below he could see the mob gazing up at him with tense, white faces. Men began running forward with a net. They seemed like marionettes in a puppet show. They spread the net beneath the window and held it taut. The limp bundle quivered and moaned and clutched at him with nervous, clawing fingers. He lifted it up to the sill and sent it down with a heave.

He was nearing the end of the gully, he felt. Heat was coming upward in great, sickening waves. He felt the joists of the window shake under his hand. The roar became deafening, like the rush of a great cataract. There was a crash that shattered his eardrums. He turned.

The centre of the floor had fallen in, and before him lay a great pool of flame that writhed and twisted and licked at the edges. He looked at it dully. Why, there was the end of the road. Right in the red heart of the pool he could see the green Sussex downs,

HARLEY JOHNSTON, GENTLEMAN

and the white sheep grazing, and the grass ripple under the breeze. And there, looking out to the sea, was a figure in white. He could see the soft brown wave of her hair, and the tan of her arms. Here was the end of the road at last, thank God! He gave a great cry of victory and leaped forward.

XV

Pretty, of the *Era*, read the two sticks that indulgent editors gave the story with a gasp. The police had got Harley's name and address from a memorandum book he had let drop when tearing off his coat. Pretty, who had been giving him what counsel he could, including that to go home, went to the rooming house to see if he could help arrange the boy's affairs.

Pretty, who was a wise man, found many things that needed explanation. There was, for instance, a tall, dark, handsome woman, whose social position Pretty could easily estimate, blinking back tears in the boy's room. There was a packet of unopened letters in a girl's hand which Pretty opened, examined cursorily, and destroyed. And then he remembered that when the net was spread for him, the boy had not jumped, and Pretty, in his wisdom, understood.

HARLEY JOHNSTON, GENTLEMAN

"My dear madam," Pretty wrote home for him, "it is very hard, I know, but there is this to remember—that your son died like a gallant gentleman, doing what you would have wished him to do had you been there. I have heard of the line of soldiers from which he has sprung, who have given their lives unselfishly for their country. Inscribe his name beside theirs, for he was a hero, too."

Another paragraph he found more difficult to write:

"There had been little news from him to you and to his fiancée for some months. He had been going through a period of disappointment and depression, a period which many young men who come here have to face. He was certainly waiting for the time when he should have something definite to report. This undoubtedly would have been very shortly, as there was nothing I was more sure of than of his ultimate success."

He thought for a moment and added:

"It may sound out of place, but I am glad to be the one to tell you of your boy's gallant end. He was a lover his fiancée may be proud of, a son to be proud of, a friend of whom we are all proud."

He folded and sealed the letter.

"I don't know who 'we' are," he said to himself, "but, by God! I am."